Megan looked slowly around the room. There was no one in it but her.

But when her eyes moved to the big oval mirror, she gasped, her hands flying to her mouth. She backed rapidly away from the mirror until she bumped into the dresser, its fat white knobs poking her rudely in the back. And there she stood, transfixed. And completely, utterly terrified.

Instead of her own image, the glass was filled with a wispy, shadowy plume, faintly purple in color, weaving gently back and forth in the glass. Gradually, as Megan continued to stare with horror-stricken eyes, the plume began to take on a vaguely human shape.

**Other Point paperbacks
you will enjoy:**

Funhouse
by Diane Hoh

Beach Party
by R. L. Stine

The Boyfriend
by R. L. Stine

The Snowman
by R. L. Stine

Teacher's Pet
by Richie Tankersley Cusick

Prom Dress
by Lael Littke

My Secret Admirer
by Carol Ellis

THE ACCIDENT

Diane Hoh

SCHOLASTIC INC.
New York Toronto London Auckland Sydney

ISBN 0-590-44330-5

Copyright © 1991 by Diane Hoh.
All rights reserved. Published by Scholastic Inc.
POINT is a registered trademark of Scholastic Inc.

12 11 10   5 6/9

Printed in the U.S.A.   01

First Scholastic printing, April 1991

Chapter 1

The heat was oppressive, settling down on the village of Lakeside, smothering it like a wet woolen blanket. A pale charcoal sky hung low over the lake and the tall pine trees surrounding the navy-blue water like giant sentries. For days the dark sky had promised, but refused to deliver, the relief of a cooling rain.

The students at Philippa Moore Senior High School in Lakeside complained constantly about the heat, unusual for the last weeks of May. "It's never this hot this early," they said, their clothing sticking to their skin like damp tissue paper.

Philippa Moore, an old but still-beautiful structure of antique brick and white pillars, was not air-conditioned. On days when heat rays radiated up from the sidewalks outside, and chalk grew moist and sticky inside, sitting in one of its classrooms was like being roasted over hot coals.

Class cutting became rampant. Even those students who seldom skipped gave in to the temptation to escape the stifling classrooms.

Jenny Winn, sixteen; her fifteen-year-old sister, Barbie; and their best friend, Cappie Cabot, cut their final class of the day on a Wednesday afternoon. "The woods on the other side of the lake will be cooler," Jenny said. "We'll go there."

They put the top down on the big old yellow convertible, a legacy from their older brother Gene when he went off to college. The car had fins that looked like wings. While tiny Jenny would have preferred a cute little sports car to tool around town in, when given the elephantine vehicle she had said, "Wheels are wheels," and had quickly learned to handle the car like an expert.

"We should have asked Megan and Hilary to come along," Cappie said as Jenny confidently guided the car down the highway. "But Megan probably wouldn't have cut, and Hilary said she had to go to the drama department after school."

"I think Megan had stuff to do for her birthday party," Barb said, her long, blonde hair blowing around her freckled face. "She's so excited about it. Wish *I* was turning sixteen."

"You will."

The big yellow car moved along the road beside the lake, creating a breeze that was thick and hot, aimed straight at them.

But they all agreed it was better than being in one of Philippa's classrooms.

"It had better be cool in the woods," Jenny muttered, easing into the curve at Sutter's Bend. "If Miss Beech finds out I deliberately cut class, she'll hang me out to dry. So this little excursion had better be worth it."

As she always did when she reached the sharp elbow in the road, Jenny eased up on her speed and kept a firm grip on the wheel. She had driven this curve hundreds of times since she got her license in January. It was part of her trip to and from school every day.

On her right lay the lake, still too cold for swimming, guarded by stately pine trees. Big old houses and smaller, rustic cabins were scattered along its shores. The woods were off to her left, and a dry open road lay ahead of her like a flat gray ribbon. There was no oncoming traffic and no one tailgating her. Taking the curve should have been as simple as brushing her teeth.

But it wasn't. When she turned the steering wheel, it moved too easily, too rapidly, too loosely. And the car refused to obey. It continued moving in a straight line. Jenny tried again, using more force this time. The steering wheel spun uselessly, as if it had nothing whatsoever to do with the car.

She hunched over the wheel, saying in a low, tense voice, "Barb, something's wrong."

Barbie glanced up, unconcerned. "What? What's the matter?" When she realized that the big yellow car wasn't following the curve, she jerked upright. "Jenny — "

Everything happened very quickly, no longer than the blink of an eye.

The car left the road, heading directly toward a

utility pole on their right. And Jenny made a bad mistake. In her panic to regain control of the car, the foot she intended for the brake pedal slammed down instead on the gas pedal.

The car shot forward.

The three girls screamed, their hands flying up instinctively to protect their faces.

The car hit the utility pole, and the sound of metal crashing into wood echoed out over the quiet, peaceful lake.

The impact sliced the pole in two. Its upper section tipped in slow motion and descended onto the crumpled pile of yellow metal. Sparks danced about as the wires came into contact with the steel and the road.

Barbie, upon impact tossed like a rag doll from the convertible, lay stunned, not quite conscious, on the grassy area above the lake, safe from the spitting wires. She was murmuring her sister's name.

The only sign of the girl whose name Barbie kept repeating was a bare and bloodied arm draped lifelessly over what was left of the driver's door. Cappie was hidden within the bent and broken car.

Then Barbie lost consciousness, and the only sound breaking the ominous silence was the faint hissing of the electrical wires.

Chapter 2

Megan Logan stood before the free-standing, oval, wooden-framed cheval mirror in her bedroom, listening to the whippoorwills outside her open window and wondering if the blue-green dress she was trying on should be shortened for her party. The bird song was nearly drowned out by the constant humming and chugging of boat engines on the lake behind her house and by the sound of the television downstairs. But Megan was very good at filtering out sounds that didn't interest her and hearing only those she chose, like the call of the whippoorwills.

The blue and cream slant-ceilinged bedroom at the rear of the house was stuffy and hot, not conducive to trying on clothes. Old houses like this one, her mother's inheritance from Megan's grandmother Martha, had no air conditioning. Normally the breeze off the water cooled the house, but during this heat wave, even the breeze was oven-warm. The silky fabric of the dress clung uncomfortably to her moist skin.

But she had to check out the dress. The Sweet

Sixteen party her parents were throwing for her was coming up soon, and there was still a lot to do.

Her parents had said, "We'll give you a big party for your sixteenth birthday, Megan, but only if you buckle down and pull up your grades."

Megan had pulled up her grades, but it hadn't been easy. It wasn't that she didn't care about school. She did. She just had trouble concentrating, that was all.

"Megan is a dreamer," her English teacher, Miss Bolt, had told her parents during their most recent conference. "She's bright enough, but she spends too much time gazing out the window. When I call on her, she always looks so surprised, as if she isn't sure exactly where she is. The thing is, she almost always knows the right answer. And *that* surprises her, too."

A stern lecture from her father had followed, and then Megan's renewed effort to pay attention in class, and now the party was in the works.

A week from Sunday she would reach that magical age: sixteen. All of her friends were excited about the party. But no one more than Megan.

In spite of the excitement, an uneasy feeling had plagued Megan all day. She had no explanation for it. Maybe it was just the heat. But at the back of her mind, she felt that *something* was wrong.

Megan surveyed the dress with a critical eye. It had to be exactly right for her Sweet Sixteen party. The party would be held here, at the big white house on the lake. Her family had moved in just three months before, after her grandmother's death.

Megan swept her thick dark hair up, away from her shoulders and held it high with one hand. The frothy mass of gentle curls, dark as crows' wings, framed her oval face and sea-green eyes. It always seemed to Megan to be a wonderful mistake. Shouldn't someone as shy and quiet as she have plain, straight, brown hair? Didn't this hair belong on someone more outgoing, more dramatic? She'd been told it was just like her grandmother Martha's had been when she was young.

Wasn't the full, short skirt of the turquoise dress half an inch too long? It might make her look shorter than she actually was. She hadn't been lucky enough to get the hair *and* height. Maybe she should buy higher heels. Justin was tall enough. Not that she'd asked him yet to be her date. But she would. Any day now. Her best friends, Hilary Bench, Jenny Winn, and Cappie Cabot, had said it was up to her to ask, because she was the guest of honor. "You get to choose," Hil had said firmly.

I choose Justin Carr, Megan thought to herself.

As if on cue, the blue telephone on the nightstand in front of her window rang, and Justin's deep voice answered her quiet hello.

"So, are you hitting the books in preparation for the bio quiz tomorrow?" he asked. "Old Ollie had that gleam in his eye today when he warned us about it. You know, that look he gets behind his glasses when he's been plotting The Attack of the Killer Quiz. Boy, how that guy loves to see us sweat!" He

7

laughed. "Sorry. Poor choice of words. Who needs help in that department now that Lakeside has become the Overpowering Inferno?"

Megan laughed. During the past year, Justin had become one of her best friends. He made her laugh. And he listened. Most boys didn't. He never teased her about preferring jazz to rock music, or for taking long walks by herself, or for being late repeatedly to the first-period science class they shared. The last time she'd come in late, walking into class sweaty and breathless, it had been because she'd stopped to pick wildflowers. When she had unthinkingly blurted out that truth to Old Ollie, the entire class had roared with laughter. Except Justin. He had smiled at her and gone to the sink at the back of the room to fill a beaker with water, which he then presented to her with a flourish. Flushing with embarrassment, Megan had thrust the black-eyed Susans into the beaker. Justin carefully installed the bouquet on his lab table, where it remained until the petals turned gray-brown and began to fall.

No one in the room had laughed when he did that. People didn't laugh at Justin. People took him seriously. Having him on her side was wonderful.

She had fallen in love with him that day.

But she still hadn't asked him to be her date for the party.

Because Justin Carr, who was tall and thin like one of the reeds in the shallower coves of the lake, Justin with his sandy, wavy hair and his gray eyes behind his wire-rimmed glasses, Justin with a smile that said, "The world's a crazy, interesting place, isn't it?" could invite any girl to any party, and that girl would be dashing out to buy a new dress before he'd even finished asking. So why would he want to go to a party with someone who was just a friend? And maybe not the most exciting friend in the world, either. Another thing she'd inherited from her grandmother Martha was shyness. She hated being shy, but there didn't seem to be anything she could do about it.

Hilary always insisted, "Justin is crazy about you, you dope. You're the only one who doesn't see it. He's just afraid of scaring you off by making a move on you. Asking him to your party will let him know how you feel. Then you can both relax."

To which Megan always replied, "Silly Hilly. We're just friends." And wished like crazy that it weren't true.

"I just opened my book a minute ago," Megan told Justin, flopping across her bed unmindful of the blue-green party dress and opening her biology book. "Are you ready for the quiz?"

Justin laughed again. "I was born ready."

"Lots of people are blowing it off." Megan rolled over onto her back. The dress rustled a protest. "There are tons of people out on the lake. I guess it's cooler out there. I'm sure I heard Karen Tucker's laugh, and she's in Ollie's class."

"Well, if she's planning on batting her eyelashes and telling him her book fell in the water and got ruined so she couldn't study, she'd better get real. Ollie isn't impressed by those sexy types."

Megan's eyes closed in pain. He thought Karen

Tucker was sexy? What was it that Karen had that she, Megan, didn't? As if I didn't know, she thought. Karen has the art of flirting down to a science and a great figure. She *is* sexy.

A siren sounded in the distance. Then another. But they were too far away to be the Lake Patrol. So it wasn't a boating accident. A fire in town? A car wreck?

That uneasy feeling she'd had all day kicked her in the stomach. Sirens meant something, some-where, was very wrong.

"Megan? You still there?"

"Listen, Justin, I can't sit here and talk to you all night." She was still stinging from the "sexy type" remark. She didn't care if he heard it in her voice. "You may have this quiz aced, but I don't. I've got to go."

"Oh. Okay." Was that disappointment in his voice? Then why didn't he say, "I'll miss you when you hang up"?

Because Justin never said stuff like that to Megan Logan. He talked to her about books and music and metaphysics and the power of the universe, but he never said, "Megan Logan, you make the sun shine for me," which happened to be exactly what she wanted to hear.

"See you at lunch tomorrow?"

"Sure," she murmured, her voice lake-water cool. "I mean, I guess so. I always do. See you at lunch, I mean." She groaned silently. Brilliant. Pos-itively brilliant. She really should see an agent about some heavy-duty public speaking. She'd make a fortune.

There was a brief silence. Then Justin asked quietly, "You okay?"

She was being stupid and childish. Justin hadn't done anything wrong. Karen Tucker *was* sexy. Everyone said so. But she still didn't feel like asking him to her party, not right now. Maybe later. "Sure. I'm fine. Just hyper about the quiz, that's all. I'd better go. See you tomorrow."

The minute she hung up, she was angry with herself for not asking him about the party. It was only eleven days away, and the birthday girl still didn't have a date.

Maybe I'll go stag, she thought, switching on her radio. But Mom would have a fit. "Honestly, Megan," she'd say in exasperation, "why didn't you ask Justin? I suppose you put it off and put it off until it was too late. What am I going to do with you?"

Gram had always defended her. Whenever Megan's parents threw up their hands in despair because their only daughter had "her head in the clouds," Gram would say mildly, "Megan marches to a different drummer, that's all. All creative people have their heads in the clouds. Maybe she'll write a great novel one day. She's fine. Leave her alone."

But Gram was gone, five months now.

Megan still missed her.

She got up, smoothing out the turquoise skirt, just as the music on her radio was replaced by an announcer's deep voice saying, *"This word just in. There has been a serious automobile accident at Sutter's Bend just west of town. Three people have been taken by Emergency Medical Services to Lakeside Medical Center after their vehicle hit a utility pole. Residents are urged to avoid the area as live wires pose a safety threat. The names of the injured, whose families have been notified, are sisters Jennifer and Barbara Winn, ages sixteen and fifteen, and Catherine Cabot, sixteen."*

Megan's hand flew to her mouth. She stood stock-still in the center of the room, frozen in shock. Jenny? And Barb? And Cappie? Hurt?

She couldn't move. The sirens had not wailed for some poor stranger, after all. They had been shrieking for three of her closest friends. And the announcer had clearly said, "A serious accident." *How* serious?

The telephone shrilled again, startling her. Numbly, she reached down and picked up the receiver.

"Meg? Megan, is that you? It's me, Hilary. Megan, *say* something!"

All the people out on the lake had gone home, leaving it peaceful and quiet. Downstairs, the television her parents and her ten-year-old brother, Thomas, were watching droned on. The whippoorwills were quiet. Everything, except the suffocating heat, was as it always was.

Except that something horrible had just happened.

"Hil," she said slowly. "Jenny and Barb . . ."

"I know. I heard. That's why I'm calling."

"What happened? Jenny's a really good driver."

"My dad thinks a tire blew. He said that when the pavement's hot as a barbecue grill for more than a few days, it's hard on tires. He said a blowout on such a big car would make it really hard for someone as tiny as Jenny to control."

"Oh, God, Hil, this is awful! Have you heard how bad they're hurt?"

"No, not yet. But it *sounds* really bad. Dad said that when wires are down at an accident, it takes longer to get the . . . the victims out. Too dangerous for emergency personnel."

"I just can't believe it, Hil!"

"And Jenny was so excited this afternoon." Hilary swallowed hard. "She'd asked Rob Lyle to your party. And he'd said yes. . . ."

Both girls fell silent, wondering if Jenny Winn would even be attending the party eleven short days away. How serious was "serious"?

"I can't talk about this anymore," Hilary said, breaking the silence. "Call me if you hear anything, okay?"

"I will. You, too."

When the blue phone was back in its cradle, Megan sat on the bed, lost in shock and disbelief. Was it really true? Had her friends smashed into a utility pole? How scared they must have been! She couldn't stand to think about them in pain, hurting, maybe scarred, maybe . . . dead? No, that couldn't be. The announcer hadn't mentioned a fatality. But "injured" was bad enough.

Shaking, she got up to remove the party dress. That made her wonder if Jenny had found "the perfect party dress" she'd been hunting for, and Megan burst into tears.

Suddenly Megan felt the temperature in her room plunge. The lights dimmed, sending the room into near-darkness, and the radio fell ominously silent.

Mouth and eyes wide open, Megan clutched at a bedpost. What was happening? An earthquake? A storm?

She was about to bolt for the door when a soft voice whispered, "Why are you crying, Megan Logan?"

Megan stopped in her tracks, unable to breathe.

The voice was faint and hollow, like the distant echo Megan's own voice returned to her when she called out across the lake late at night.

"I said, why are you crying?"

Chapter 3

Megan looked slowly around the room. There was no one in it but her.

But when her eyes moved to the big oval mirror, she gasped, her hands flying to her mouth. She backed rapidly away from the mirror until she bumped into the dresser, its fat white knobs poking her rudely in the back. And there she stood, transfixed. And completely, utterly terrified.

Instead of her own image, the glass was filled with a wispy, shadowy plume, faintly purple in color, weaving gently back and forth in the glass. Gradually, as Megan continued to stare with horror-stricken eyes, the plume began to take on a vaguely human shape. There were no facial features, only a bright golden glow where a person's eyes, nose, and mouth would normally be. No arms or legs were apparent on the gauzy purple stream. It was like looking at a person from a great distance through a sheer, delicate veil.

I've fallen asleep, I'm having a nightmare, Megan told herself to silence her galloping heart.

"I asked why you were crying. You look very sad."

Megan was freezing. The air coming in the window behind her was toaster-warm, yet within her room, it was as cold as an underground cavern. Every inch of her body was paralyzed with fear.

Megan struggled to find her voice. "What's going on?" she whispered. "What's happening?"

An eerie silvery glow began to surround the lavender plume, lighting it from behind. "I need to talk to you, Megan Logan. Don't be scared. I won't hurt you."

"Who . . . what are you?" Megan croaked hoarsely. Her legs weren't going to hold her up much longer. She felt that at any second she was going to collapse to the floor, completely helpless. Willing herself to remain upright, she repeated shakily, "What *are* you?"

The answer came softly, sweetly. "I am Juliet."

Megan had spent countless hours sitting on the terrace roof shaded by the branches of the huge old oak tree. There she watched the clouds drifting in over the lake. She always found something interesting in each wad of cottony white, each slab of pale or dark gray, each sunset-pinked gossamer trail.

But now, staring in terror at the shapeless, wavy stream of lavender in her mirror, she saw nothing familiar, nothing ordinary, nothing to still her hammering heart. The only thing she could be sure of was that the voice coming from the wispy column was, like her own, feminine.

"Juliet? But . . . but . . ." Megan sank down on the bed, shivering. The room was so cold. Yet a stream of stultifying, breath-defying hot air continued to crawl in sluggishly through her open window.

This wasn't happening. This *can't* be happening, Megan thought.

The voice was soft as cobwebs. "You think I shouldn't have a name?"

Without taking her eyes off the mirror, Megan slowly reached out and pulled the comforter from her bed, wrapping herself in it. The lighting in the room remained dim, while the silvery glow in the mirror seemed to deepen. "Go away," Megan whispered. "Whoever — whatever you are, I don't want you here. You don't belong here."

"I can't. I've got to talk to you, Megan. And you've got to listen to me. It's important."

"No," Megan said in a mere whisper. She wanted to cry out for her parents, or her brother, but she knew the shout would never escape her frozen throat. "I don't want to."

Sadness sounded in the voice, and bitter disappointment. "You won't listen to me? No, oh, no, that can't be! I was sure you would. I've waited so long. So very long . . ." The voice trailed off, the silvery glow began to dim.

"You've waited? For me?" Confusion added to Megan's fear. "Where? Where did you wait? Where did you come from?"

"I come from another time, another place. I'm here now, that's all that matters."

"How did you get into that mirror?"

The voice gathered strength as Megan began to respond. The silvery light throbbed, brightening again. "The mirror isn't important. It doesn't mean anything. I'm only using it so you can see me."

"But I don't *want* to see you!" Megan cried. "I don't want you here! Just go away!"

"Please, Megan, please, all I ask is that you listen. It would mean so much to me."

Only the possibility that she had fallen asleep and was caught in a horrible nightmare kept Megan from fleeing the room. That, and the mesmerizing quality of the plume's plaintive voice as it begged her to listen.

"You're getting ready for your party?" the voice said. "Pretty dress."

Megan said nothing.

"You're wondering how I know about your birthday. I know because it's my birthday, too. We share that. That's one of the reasons I can talk with you. But we weren't born in the same year."

Megan was seized by a fresh chill. The thing in the mirror had had a birthday? It had once been born, had lived, had maybe been a young girl like Megan?

But . . . if that was what it had *been*, what was it *now*?

Struggling, she managed to ask, "When? When *were* you born?"

"Nineteen thirty."

"Nineteen thirty?" Sixty-one years ago. But the voice was not that of a sixty-one-year-old woman. It was as young as Megan's.

"That dress really is pretty."

Megan looked down in surprise, as if someone had slipped the dress on her when she wasn't looking. The blue-green skirt peeked out from beneath the blue print comforter.

They had both been speaking in near-whispers, but now, the voice in the mirror gained strength. "I had a new dress for my sixteenth birthday party, too," it added wistfully. "My dress was blue like yours, but a darker shade, like the night sky. It was taffeta. It crackled when I walked. I loved that sound. I was having an orchestra at my party, and colored lanterns strung above the lawn, and napkins with my initials on them."

Megan was clenching her fists so tightly around the comforter, her knuckles looked bleached. The . . . thing in the mirror had had a birthday party?

Suddenly the plume became very agitated, jerking erratically from side to side. "But I never had my party," the voice said mournfully. "It was canceled."

A wave of skin-scorching heat blew in Megan's window, but she scarcely noticed. The agitation in the mirror terrified her. It . . . the plume . . . Juliet . . . was becoming very upset. I should leave, she thought numbly. I should run, right now, get out of this room. But fear had turned her body to stone.

An anguished sob filled the room. "There was an accident. A bad one."

The light around the plume dimmed, and the room became lost in shadow. An owl in the oak tree beside the terrace hooted. Megan jumped, startled by the sound. She spoke automatically, as if in a trance. "An accident?"

"A boating accident. Out there on the lake, in that cove just around the bend. Do you know the place?"

Megan knew it well. Most lake people avoided it because of the rocks, some jutting up above the water, most hidden beneath it. At the bottom of the lake there was a treacherous tangle of undergrowth and weeds lying in wait to imprison whatever might come its way. The cove had a history of boat wrecks and drownings.

Was this . . . Juliet . . . saying she was a part of that tragic history?

Megan waited with growing dread. Something terrible had happened to the thing in the mirror. She knew it. She didn't want to know what that something terrible was.

"Our boat hit a rock. I hadn't had time to learn to swim, but it wouldn't have helped. I was thrown overboard and knocked unconscious. My body became tangled in the undergrowth. By the time I was pulled from the water . . . it was too late. . . .

"I never made it to my party," the voice whispered sadly. "But . . . it was all a long time ago. Forty-six years ago. Such a long time . . ."

When Megan still said nothing, the thing called Juliet added, "I would have been sixteen the day of my party. Like you, Megan. Sweet sixteen . . ."

The wispy plume began spinning like a top. Soft, anguished sobs filled the room with pure pain. "I'd been planning that party for ages. I was sure it meant all the fun would begin. The best time of my life. I was pretty and very popular." The spinning stopped, but the voice was heavy with distress. "Everyone said I had so much promise. But that horrid accident took my life from me before I ever had a chance to live it."

Megan was struck by the horror of Juliet's words. Fresh tears streamed down her face, and her eyes were full of pain. "No, oh, no," Megan whispered. Then, lifting her head, she said, "But this isn't happening. This is *not* happening."

"Oh, dear, I've made you cry again. I shouldn't have upset you. I'll leave now, but I'll come back another time. Thank you for listening to me. . . . Most people wouldn't have."

And before Megan could cry out, the light dimmed, went out, and the mirror was clear again. There was nothing in it but the reflection of a girl, shaking violently beneath a blue print quilt, her face streaked with tears.

The lights came up to full power, and the radio came back on, as if Juliet had flicked a switch as she left. Once again, the room became suffocatingly hot.

Megan trembled for a long time. After a while, she removed the comforter, took off the party dress, and hung it carefully on a hanger in her closet. She got ready for bed, moving the entire time in stunned slow-motion. When she crawled up underneath the canopy, she pulled the pale blue sheet up over her in spite of the suffocating heat, unable to shake the chill left by the wraith in her mirror and the words the wraith had spoken.

I dreamed the whole thing, she told herself, staring up at the yellowed ceiling. I'm dreaming right now. I'm dreaming that I'm just going to bed, when the truth is, I've been asleep for hours.

The thought was comforting. It allowed her to relax and go to sleep.

The next morning when she awoke and remembered, her eyes flew to the mirror.

Except for Megan's own sleepy-eyed, tousle-haired reflection, the mirror was empty.

Chapter 4

On Thursday morning, Lakeside residents awoke to disappointment. The sky was still a sullen gray, the sun hidden, the heat still suffocating the town.

Megan felt like she'd slept in a sauna. Her head ached, her skin felt sticky, and her hair was matted to her head.

After checking the mirror and finding it empty, she thought immediately of her friends. Were they okay? She hoped her parents had heard something. Maybe her mother had talked to someone at the hospital.

As she got ready for school, her eyes returned repeatedly to the big mirror. Although there was nothing there, the feeling of a foreign presence lingered in the room. Something that didn't belong had entered her room, uninvited. It was gone now, but the sense of it remained.

But I *did* dream that whole thing, she told herself after her shower. She pulled on white shorts and a pale yellow top. I dreamed it because I was so upset about the accident that nearly killed three of my friends. So I dreamed about someone my age who *had* died in an accident.

It had been so real, though. She remembered clearly every second of it. Slipping her feet into a pair of sandals, she pulled her thick mass of curls into a ponytail and fastened it with a yellow clip. Her morning shower had done nothing to ease the headache. The pounding behind her eyes was relentless.

Megan deliberately kept her back to the free-standing mirror as she halfheartedly applied a touch of blush and mascara. But as she left the room, her biology book in her arms, her blue denim shoulder bag hanging from one wrist, she couldn't resist glancing one more time into the wooden-framed glass.

There was nothing in it but the reflection of a pale-faced girl in yellow and white. I look like a wilted daisy, Megan thought in disgust. When she closed the bedroom door behind her, she hoped she was closing out all memory of the strange wraith and its tragic story. And she hoped that when she came home later that day, her room would feel like her own again.

The early-morning mist on the water had already cleared as Megan pedaled her bicycle to school, using the bike path above the lake. Glancing up at the granite-colored sky, she told herself it was going to be another skin-sticky day. Everyone at school would be moaning and groaning about the weather.

Unless they were preoccupied with last night's accident.

Megan crossed the highway to Philippa Moore High School, where groups of teenagers in shorts and tank tops milled about on the lawn. Her mother hadn't had any news about the physical condition of her friends. She had found out only that they were all still alive. Locking her bicycle in the rack beneath the huge flagpole, Megan quickly searched for someone who could give her more information about Jenny, Barb, and Cappie.

But no one knew anything until lunch period, when Megan met Justin and Hilary and learned that Hilary had called the hospital and talked to Mrs. Winn.

"Barb's okay," she told Megan and Justin. "She was thrown clear and landed on grass. She's going home today. Cappie has a broken wrist and a lot of bruises. But Jenny wasn't so lucky. She has a really awful head injury, and her collarbone was shattered. There weren't any seat belts in the car because it was so old. Mr. Winn had ordered some, but they hadn't come in yet." Hilary paused, then added quietly, "Mrs. Winn was crying the whole time we were talking."

Megan shuddered. Her nasty headache persisted. My friends could all have been killed, she told herself, believing it for the first time. They could have died.

Like poor Juliet.

Except Juliet wasn't real. She was just a dream. An awful dream.

25

What was almost worse than the dream was the feeling now that she was being watched. She felt eyes on her, following her every move. Her skin itched. It had started when she walked up the school steps, and it stayed with her. She had to keep fighting the urge to glance over her shoulder. When she did look around nervously, no one was paying any attention to her.

The student body at Philippa Moore was sprawled across the back lawn on the embankment sloping down to the lake. The air was thick and sluggish, making any sort of movement an effort. Too wiped out by the suffocating heat to play volleyball or toss a Frisbee, everyone studied or talked softly while they ate.

But the disturbed quiet across campus had nothing to do with the heat. It was the direct result of three of their own narrowly escaping death. The students were trying to deal with the grim fact of the accident.

"I don't get it," Justin said. "Jenny's a good driver, and it wasn't raining yesterday. No slippery roads. Anybody hear how it happened?"

Hilary, sitting on the ground with her legs crossed, leaned forward. Her thick, straight blonde hair was cut short and square around her ears in a shining cap, her round face pink-cheeked and healthy looking. "Mrs. Winn told me that when they hit that curve, Jenny aimed the car around it just like she always did. At least she tried to. But nothing happened. Barbie told her mother that the car just wouldn't turn. It went straight into that utility pole like it had a mind of its own."

"Sounds like the steering went," Justin commented.

Hilary shrugged. "Maybe. Mrs. Winn said the sheriff is checking out the car."

Justin frowned. His sandy hair curled softly across his forehead. He was wearing khaki shorts and a white short-sleeved T-shirt. His warm gray eyes were pensive behind his wire-rimmed glasses. "Jenny could be out of commission for a long time. She's going to go stir-crazy in that hospital."

"Well," Megan said, "as soon as she can have visitors, we'll just have to see that she doesn't get lonely."

Justin smiled at her. "If anybody can cheer her up, you can. You're good at that."

"Well, I think it all stinks!" Hilary complained. "School's almost over, and Jenny won't get to finish out the year."

After a moment or two of somber silence, Hilary sat up straighter and said, "Let's not talk about this anymore. Too depressing." She made a face of disgust as she said, "Guess who asked me out this morning?" Hilary could switch moods as easily as she changed a T-shirt.

"Who?" Justin asked. "Who do we know without a single shred of taste?"

Hilary crossed her eyes at him. "Donny Richardson. He asked me to a movie. Isn't that a hoot?"

"What did you tell him?" Megan asked, knowing

perfectly well that short, squat, mustached Donny was definitely not Hilary's type. He wasn't tall enough or cute enough. He wasn't athletic, and he wasn't popular. Definitely not Hilary Bench's type.

"I said, 'Not in this lifetime.' The guy has the personality of a hangnail."

"Hilary, did you have to be so cruel?" Megan asked. It wasn't hard to imagine the pain of that kind of rejection. If Justin ever treated her like that, she'd die. "You could have been a little bit nicer."

"If you're polite with guys like Donny, they never give up."

"Well," Justin said, "I think you could have been more tactful." He grinned. "Although we know that tact isn't among your limited virtues, Bench. Donny's not a bad guy, and the girls in this school treat him like dirt. He probably has his limits, like everyone else. I was with Jenny a couple of weeks ago when Donny asked her to a movie. She turned him down. She was more polite than you, Hil, but he stomped off down the hall like he was squashing bugs. He was *not* happy."

Megan frowned. "He asked Jenny out? Jenny Winn?"

"Yeah."

"I think he asked Cappie out, too," Hilary said. "I saw them arguing in the hall last week. Donny yelled something about girls who say they have to wash their hair when anyone with eyes can see their hair isn't the least bit dirty." Hilary grinned. "I thought it was pretty funny." The grin disappeared.

"Now I'm not so sure." Her blue eyes narrowed.

"I feel sorry for Donny," Megan said. "Nobody likes him, and I think his home life stinks. His parents are divorced, and he moves back and forth between two different homes. That can't be much fun."

"My parents are divorced, too," Hilary said airily, "but I'm not a dweeb like Donny."

"Sure you are," Justin said lazily, grinning. "You're just prettier than Donny."

"It must be awful to be so unpopular," Megan said slowly. She was remembering the dream, hearing Juliet say again that she'd been popular. Donny wasn't. But he was still luckier than Juliet had been. He just didn't know it.

"Oh, Megan," Hilary said in exasperation, "You're always feeling *sorry* for people! You just don't get it that there are some really crummy people out there who don't have good excuses for the rotten way they act. Get with the program, will you?"

"But that's what makes her so lovable," Justin said lightly, giving Megan's arm a reassuring squeeze. "That's part of her charm."

Megan smiled up at him. Hilary made a gagging gesture, but she grinned as she did it.

Before they went back into school, Megan turned and looked back at the lawn. No one seemed to be paying any particular attention to her. So why did she have this feeling that she was a specimen under a microscope? It gave her goose bumps.

Later, passing Donny Richardson in the hall on her way to art class, she found herself smiling at him with more warmth than usual.

He looked surprised, and his skinny black mustache remained in place, refusing to curve into a return smile. Megan had a feeling that even if he had smiled, it wouldn't have reached his eyes. They seemed so cold and empty.

When she reached the art room, she went straight to her assigned cubbyhole at the rear of the room. There was a square of red construction paper sticking halfway out, sandwiched between her latest drawing and her box of pastels.

She hadn't used red construction paper lately.

Curious, she slid the paper out of the cubbyhole and looked at it. What she saw was a crude, childish drawing of a large yellow car with no top, filled with a strange cargo.

Megan walked over to the big window to look at the picture in better light.

It was horrible. Seated in the driver's seat of the crudely drawn car was a . . . horse? Wearing a string of pink beads around its throat. On the passenger's side of the front seat sat what looked like a large candy bar beside a fat yellow-and-black-striped blob with wings. A bumblebee.

What on earth . . . ?

Her eyes moved to the backseat. A hat of some kind was drawn there. It had a visor with an emblem on it. A baseball cap? There was a small, green ball beside it. A green baseball? No. It looked more like an oversized green pea.

As people began to file into the big art room, Megan studied the picture carefully. It was a simple puzzle. The car was clearly Jenny's. The candy bar and the bumblebee were easy: Bar. Bee. Barbie. And the cap and the pea meant Cappie. But why was there a horse in the driver's seat?

What kind of twisted mind would draw such a sick picture about a tragic accident?

And why was it in Megan's cubbyhole?

Was it a joke? If it was, someone at Philippa had a very bizarre sense of humor.

Shivering, Megan crumpled the picture angrily and tossed it into the wastebasket.

On her way out of class fifty minutes later, Megan plucked the wrinkled drawing from the trash and stuffed it into her notebook. She didn't know why she did it. She only knew that it seemed like a good idea.

When she got home, Megan approached her bedroom door with hesitation, wondering nervously if the room would still feel strange. It had been almost a whole day since the dream. Her bedroom should feel like her own room again by now.

Megan slowly pulled the door open. Instead of closing it behind her, she stood in the doorway, listening, and searching all four corners with her eyes. The room, its flowered wallpaper faded and peeling slightly in spots, would ordinarily be filled with sunshine at this time of day, but because of the slate-colored sky, it looked dreary and gray.

Megan's searching eyes found nothing out of the ordinary. The unmade bed seemed to hold no secrets, the lace curtains hanging from her canopy and on her windows waited patiently for her to enter the room, and the clothes lying on the floor in small, scattered heaps were as familiar as the stuffed animals cluttering the white shelves at the far end of the room.

Megan stepped inside and closed the door.

At last, she let herself glance into the full-length mirror.

It was empty.

Of course it is, she told herself, and went to her desk to remove a sheaf of papers from a drawer.

She had just turned around, papers in hand, when the curtains began blowing wildly and she was hit by a blast of frigid air. Her room darkened and became shrouded in shadow.

"What are you doing, Megan Logan? Is it something fun?"

Chapter 5

Shivering with renewed fear, Megan forced her eyes to the mirror.

Juliet had returned.

I wasn't dreaming after all, Megan thought, her breath frozen in her throat. She sank down on the bed, drawing the comforter around her against the chill. "What . . . what are you *doing* here?" she whispered.

"I came to talk. Will you listen, Megan Logan? Please?"

The gauzy purple image became sharper. The head was wide at the top, narrow at the bottom, the eye sockets sunken and lit by a golden glow, the body no more than a transparent stream of lavender waving about in the glass.

While the light in the mirror grew brighter, the room itself became murky with shadows, a dark, icy place unknown to Megan. She wanted desperately to leave it, but she was afraid. And beneath the fear, curiosity stirred.

"Why are you here?" she asked softly. "You don't belong here."

"Why can't you accept me?" the voice asked. "I'm not going to hurt you."

"Leave me alone. You're scaring me."

Someone outside on the lake laughed. Megan wished fiercely that she could suddenly, magically, be transported out there to join them.

"Well, I'm not trying to scare you. I thought you'd talk to me because you have an open mind. I know that about you. I know everything about you. When I found out that we shared a birthday, I knew that I'd have to know everything. So I studied you carefully."

Megan remembered the feeling of being under a microscope. "You . . . you've been watching me?"

"I had to. When I found out that you were a dreamer, I knew that would make it easier for you to hear me."

If only she were daydreaming now. Because Megan didn't want this . . . thing . . . this Juliet . . . to be real.

"I've been waiting forever for someone who could hear me," Juliet said, her voice excited. "I can't talk to just anyone. Has to be someone exactly my age. Someone near the lake, where I died. Someone with an open mind and a kind heart. Someone with imagination and a belief that anything's possible. Someone just like you, Megan Logan." The plume waved gently back and forth in the mirror, illuminated in the darkened room only by the strange silvery glow surrounding it. "But I made myself wait to talk to you, so you'd have time to settle into this house. I was scared that if I showed up too soon, I'd frighten you off." Juliet hesitated, then added, "This was your grandmother's house. Martha's house. She left it to your mother when she died a while ago."

How could . . . Juliet . . . know so much about her? All Megan knew about the thing in her mirror was that it had lived, and died, and it was lonely.

A sigh echoed from the mirror. "It's been hard not to give up hope! All this time . . ."

Nervously fingering the edges of the comforter, Megan asked, "Hope of what?"

"Of having someone to talk with. Of reaching someone. Of . . . trading."

Mesmerized by Juliet's velvety voice, Megan failed to notice that her own body had stopped trembling, her hands were no longer shaking, and the lump in her throat had dissolved. "Trading? Trading what?"

"Nothing. Never mind. Let's talk about your party."

"But . . . you can't be here. This can't be happening." Megan's voice was remarkably steady. "How did you *get* here?"

"It was easy. I *had* to be here. You're my only chance."

"But it's . . . it's not possible."

"Anything is possible, Megan. You believe that, don't you? Isn't that what your grandmother Martha always said?"

It was. Gram had said, "Believe in everything, Megan, until you learn otherwise. Anything is possible in this world. You remember that."

But had she been talking about wispy columns of smoke in a mirror? What would she say about this visit from Juliet? Megan knew the answer to that question. Gram would say, "Do whatever you think is right, Megan. Trust yourself. Make up your own mind."

Like snow on a sun-warmed slope, the icy, mind-numbing fear began slowly, slowly, to melt away from Megan. As it ebbed, it was replaced by complete bewilderment.

Megan shifted on the bed, remembering suddenly how long ago Juliet had . . . died. "Did you . . . did you know my grandmother? Before . . . before your accident, I mean."

"Everyone knew the Logan family."

Realizing that Juliet had known her grandmother stirred an inner warmth in Megan. She had more in common with the image in her mirror than just a shared birthday. "What was she like when she was a teenager?"

"I didn't know her very well. I wasn't here, on the lake, that long. I think she was like you. Quiet, dreamy." The voice lowered, heavy again with sadness. "How I envy you, Megan! You'll have the wonderful party I never had. You'll get to live those years full of fun. Parties, dances, boyfriends . . . I missed all of that."

Tears pooled in Megan's eyes. Jenny Winn, Barb, and Cappie; all had nearly lost their lives, like this . . . like Juliet. What would that be like, to have your life end so young? The thought made her pull the comforter more closely around her, as if it could somehow protect her from harsh reality.

"Are you cold, Megan?"

"No. Just feeling sad. It . . . it isn't fair that your life ended . . . so early."

"You're nice. I knew you'd understand. I think it was unfair, too. That's why I can't be at peace. . . ." the voice moaned. "If only . . . no, never mind. You're not ready. It's too soon."

Megan frowned. "If only what?"

The light around the plume deepened, easing the shadows surrounding Megan. "Well, I really think you need more time. But since I don't have much, I'll go ahead and explain. I know you won't understand right away, but maybe after you've thought about it, we can talk again."

Megan stirred. "Understand what?"

"My life ended too soon, Megan. That's not ever supposed to happen. But I have a chance to make up for that now. If I can find someone who shares a birthday with me, and if that person can hear me, I can ask her to switch places with me for just one short week. I can ask for her willing consent to let me live her life for seven days and seven nights. That's what I want to ask of you."

Megan could not take in what she was hearing. Juliet's words whirled round and round in her head. Trade places? With . . . with *that*?

Megan felt the darkened room begin to spin around her. The dark shadows began to move, to reach out for her with cold, clammy fingers. Instinctively she pushed backward on her bed until her back was pressed up against the headboard and she could go no further. "What," she whispered hoarsely, "are you talking about?"

"It's really easy, Megan." Juliet's voice became stronger. "And it would only be for a week. A week when I'd have the chance to live the most fun time in a girl's life. Compared to a lifetime, a week really isn't much. But it would be enough for me. At the end of the week, I'd go away. I'd be at peace then, forever."

Megan was unable to speak. Not a muscle moved, not an eyelash blinked as she sat frozen under the canopy of her bed. The room grew deathly quiet.

"Megan?" Juliet said finally. "Megan?"

But Megan could not find her voice.

"I've scared you. I'm sorry. I knew I shouldn't have told you so soon. But I don't have very much time. Just think about it, please? Remember, Megan, *anything is possible*. I'll come back again, after you've had time to think. Thank you for listening to me."

The light in the mirror faded and vanished. Megan was alone.

She sat on the bed and stared at the wooden-framed glass. The voice had been real. Juliet had been real. Nothing had been imagined or dreamed. Even for someone like Megan, who created stories out of images she saw in clouds, it was difficult to accept. But she *had* accepted Juliet's presence.

Yet what Juliet had proposed was so strange and frightening that Megan could barely believe it. Could something like that actually be possible?

Megan had never had any trouble following her grandmother's advice: "Believe in everything until you learn otherwise." But this was too strange, too crazy to think about.

After wrestling with it for hours, the only thing Megan was sure of was that something *had* been in her mirror.

All evening, she waited for something more to happen. She couldn't read or study or concentrate on television. And she couldn't seem to move from her room.

But nothing happened.

The glass remained glass, nothing more.

Chapter 6

When Hilary called later, it was easy for Megan to keep silent about Juliet. One word about her and practical-minded Hilary would think Megan was losing her marbles.

Fortunately Hilary had other things on her mind. "Jenny's regained consciousness," she told Megan. "They think she's going to be okay. My mom talked to Mrs. Winn today. But . . . the worst thing, Megan, is that it wasn't an accident. Somebody screwed up the steering on Jenny's car."

Megan inhaled sharply. Someone had deliberately tried to hurt her friends? "Hilary, are you sure?"

"Sheriff Toomey's sure. My parents are really freaked-out. Three of my best friends are in the hospital, so my mom thinks I might be next. I could be grounded forever. She says, 'Better safe than sorry.' "

"This is unreal," Megan breathed. "Who would do something so horrible?"

"Maybe a rejected boyfriend? Like the famous

Donny Richardson, for instance? Practically every girl in school has turned him down lately. Maybe he hates all of us. And doesn't he work in his brother's garage? It has to be someone who knows auto mechanics."

"Hilary, practically everyone at Philippa took auto mechanics, including most of the girls."

Hilary's voice became testy. "Well, I don't know about you, Megan, but when *I* took it, I certainly didn't learn how to kill someone by sabotaging a car!"

When Megan had hung up, she focused on Hilary's final remarks about how lucky Jenny was. "At least she's alive," she'd said.

Unlike poor Juliet, Megan thought, flinching in pain as she pictured a fifteen-year-old girl being thrown from a boat and sinking rapidly into the deep, dark waters of the lake.

What was really tough to swallow was the horrifying news Hilary had given her. Someone had deliberately caused the car wreck? Whoever it was couldn't possibly have known the three girls would survive. The tampering had been intended to kill.

Suddenly Megan remembered the crude crayon drawing of the yellow car and its weird cargo. It was still in her notebook. She had thought of it as a cruel, sick joke. Now she realized it had been more than that.

I cut art on Tuesday, she remembered. Hilary talked me into a spur-of-the-moment trip to the mall. I never checked my cubbyhole that day. It could have been in there then, before the accident ever happened. Which would make it *not* a cruel joke but . . . a warning.

If she took the drawing to Sheriff Toomey, would he laugh? He was a nice man, but if she brought him evidence that looked like a child's drawing, he might think she was wasting his time. She would have to think about it.

Exhausted, Megan began getting ready for bed.

Lost in worry, she had just slipped into a pair of white shortie pajamas when the temperature in her room plummeted again. She wrapped a blanket around her shoulders and turned to face the mirror. It began to glow, and Juliet took shape.

"Megan. I hope what I told you before didn't upset you. You've been so nice, listening to me."

Still wary, Megan sat on the floor in front of the mirror. "What do you want from me?" she asked cautiously. "I hope you don't think I'm going to do that . . . trading thing that you talked about."

"You won't even consider it?" Juliet asked sadly. "But I thought you had an open mind, Megan. I thought you believed anything was possible, as Martha did."

Megan shook her head vigorously. "Not that. Not . . . what you said — about trading. I don't believe *that's* possible." I don't *want* it to be, she added silently.

"Oh, but it is! And it's so simple."

"Simple how?" Megan asked suspiciously.

"You would step into the mirror, and I would step out. As you. What could be simpler?"

"It can't be that easy!"

Juliet sighed deeply. "All of the hard parts come first, Megan. Finding someone near the lake who shares my birthday. Getting her to listen. Almost no one will listen. And getting her consent to switch is the hardest thing of all. People are too afraid of the unknown."

"That's for sure," Megan agreed. The thought of becoming, even temporarily, what Juliet was — a smoky, incandescent purple plume — made her flesh feel as if a thousand tiny spiders were making their home on her skin.

"It would only be for a week, Megan," the voice pleaded. "And it's not so bad in my world. . . . You wouldn't need to worry about stubbing a toe or catching cold. Nothing from your world could touch you."

Right then, that sounded kind of appealing to Megan. "But . . . if you would look like me, does that mean I would look . . . like you?"

"You wouldn't have any physical form at all. I'm only like this so you can see me. I would be able to hear you, and you could talk to me at any time. But no one else would see or hear you."

Megan shook her head again. She would become invisible? "It's just too strange, Juliet. You need someone braver than me."

"You *are* brave, Megan, or you wouldn't have heard me in the first place. Oh, Megan, I thought you understood, I can't use anyone else. Only you. Because you live here. Because of our shared birthday. And because you listened to me."

The sadness and yearning in Juliet's voice touched Megan to the core. She thought again how horrible it would be to have your life cut short at such a young age. Wasn't that, after all, what everyone at school had been thinking about? That it could have been *their* car, their accident, and that they might not have been so lucky. They might not have survived.

As Juliet hadn't.

"Don't you believe that anything is possible?" Juliet asked. "I thought you did."

Megan remembered Hilary's phone call then. "Even if I were willing, which I'm not," she said, "this would be the wrong time to trade places with me. Someone deliberately hurt some of my friends. My best friend Hilary's mother thinks Hil might be next, but it could be me. *I* could be next. If we did this . . . trading thing, you'd be putting yourself in my place. That's not a good place to be right now."

"I don't have any choice!" Juliet's voice took on a note of desperation. "You have to be my *exact* age — fifteen. So even one minute past your sixteenth birthday is too late for me. We only have until the clock strikes midnight on Saturday. Unless I get your consent before then, my one perfect chance will disappear. I don't get another chance. If you won't help, I'll disappear forever, and I'll never know peace. So the danger you talk about doesn't matter to me. I'm willing to take that risk."

"But what about me?" Megan asked. "If I decided to trade with you and something bad happened to my body while you were in it, what would become of me?"

"Actually, Megan, you'll be safer. I can sense evil in people. I'd never let anyone like that get close enough to hurt me. So you wouldn't have to worry."

Megan sat up very straight. "You mean . . . you mean you would know who hurt Jenny?"

"I think so. I can't promise. But I think so."

If Juliet could identify the cruel, sick person who had sabotaged Jenny's car and created the twisted picture, Lakeside could return to its normal, peaceful way of life.

Megan sat, lost in thought, while Juliet said nothing more. She was Juliet's *only* chance at getting back one short week of the lifetime she'd missed? There was no one else? What had happened to Juliet was horrible, tragic, and so unfair. No one should die so young. It wasn't right, it just wasn't right at all.

"Maybe I'll think about it," she said finally. That scared her so much, she added hastily, "But that's a *maybe*, understand?"

The plume began dancing with excitement. "Oh, of course, Megan. *Maybe* gives me hope. When my father said *maybe*, he almost always meant *yes*. But please," the soft voice begged, "use your open mind and your kind heart, okay? I'll come back when you've had time to think. Good night, Megan. And thank you, thank you for listening."

Megan sat at the window, looking out over the lake, for a long while. But every time she started to think about Juliet's proposal, she had to put it out of her mind. It was too scary to think about at night. Maybe tomorrow . . .

When she finally got up and crawled into bed, she slept poorly. Her grandmother's voice echoed in her dreams. "Anything is possible, Megan, you remember that."

She tossed and turned all night, her nightclothes and hair soaked with sweat.

The next morning, on the way to school, Megan tried talking to Justin about Juliet.

"Justin," she began cautiously, as she climbed into his car, "what do you think happens to a person, well, after they die? Do you think their spirit stays around?"

Justin looked over at Megan. "Those are pretty strange questions. Thinking about Jenny's accident?"

"Well, it's just . . . something weird is going on at my house."

"At *your* house!" he exclaimed as he pulled away from the curb. "Listen, your house is probably the only place in town where weird things *aren't* happening. Someone screwing up Jenny's steering, now *that's* weird!"

"Justin, I — "

"So tell me something," he interrupted, "do you think Donny's behind this stuff? Richardson?"

Maybe it was just as well Justin was distracted today, Megan thought. If she told him about Juliet, he might start to think she was really flaky. He'd told her once that she wasn't like other girls because she listened. *Really* listened, he'd said. That ·was fine. She'd been flattered. But being "different" because she was a good listener was one thing. Seeing purple plumes in her mirror was something else. Justin might think she was just plain weird. She wouldn't tell him. Not yet. Maybe never.

"I don't know," she answered thoughtfully. "I don't think so. I told him no when he asked me out, and nothing bad has happened to me."

Justin swivelled his head to look at her in surprise. "Donny asked you out? You didn't say anything about that when Hilary was talking about him yesterday."

Megan fidgeted on the seat. "Hil would have made a big deal out of it. And it wasn't a big deal. He asked me out and I said, 'No, thanks.' "

Justin's sandy eyebrows met in a frown. "How did he take it?"

"Okay, I guess."

"Look, just steer clear of him, okay? His alphabet might be missing some of its letters."

"Justin," she said, remembering the strange drawing, "have you ever heard of any famous horse named Jenny? A champion racer, maybe?"

After thinking for a minute, Justin said, "No. Why?"

She told him about the drawing, and when they parked in front of school, she showed it to him. "I figured out Barbie and Cappie," she said, "but why is the horse where Jenny should be?"

"That's not a horse," he said. "Look at the ears.

It's a mule. And it's wearing a necklace. Nice touch. Know what a female mule is called?"

"A jenny?"

"Right. Where did you get this, Megan?"

She explained. But before they could discuss it, the first-period warning bell rang.

"Meet me at the *Scribe* office after school," Justin said as they hurried to class. *The Scribe* was Philippa's newspaper. Justin was its editor. "Don't forget. We'll talk about your artist friend then."

The feeling of being watched slipped over her again, as chilling as a wet sweater. She tried ignoring it, in vain. Yet each time she glanced around, no one seemed to be paying the slightest bit of attention to her.

At lunch without Justin, who'd had an errand to run, Hilary said with disgust, "Guess who's back?" She unwrapped a strange-looking sandwich, brown and unidentifiable. Hilary was into health food. "That viper, Vicki Deems! The snake only got one week's suspension for cheating on that Spanish test. I was hoping they'd suspend her for life!"

"Just ignore her. She's not in any of your classes, is she?"

"She's in my *life*, Megan. She makes my skin crawl. I know Ken Waters was going to take me to your party. He hadn't asked me yet, but I could tell. One look at Tricki Vicki in that red halter top she's glued into and Hilary Bench is history."

Megan sipped slowly from her milk container. She didn't want Vicki Deems at her party. Maybe I'm just jealous, she thought as she peeled a banana.

Vicki is sexy, sophisticated, everything I'm not. Thank goodness Justin isn't interested in that type.

Or was he? Hadn't he called Karen Tucker "sexy"? Compared to Vicki Deems, Karen was Snow White.

But it wasn't jealousy that made Megan nervous around Vicki. It was the way those cold, dark eyes looked at a boy that made Megan shiver: black spider eyes spotting a nice, juicy fly. No wonder Vicki had no girlfriends. She had only boyfriends, and plenty of them.

After school, Megan went to the art room to check her cubbyhole, just in case.

She found another drawing.

Her stomach lurched. This one was on dark blue paper. The drawing itself was nothing more than a simple curved line, in bright pink crayon, like a giant bump on the paper. It went up and curved back down. That was all. It looked like a mound or . . . a hill.

A hill. Hilary!

Megan raced to the auditorium, where Hilary and two boys from the lighting crew were tying up loose ends after last week's junior class play.

Breathless, her heart pounding furiously in her chest, Megan was running down the wide center aisle in the auditorium when her best friend since sixth grade leaned out over the catwalk high above the stage to retrieve a loose rope.

And fell.

Chapter 7

Megan and Hilary screamed simultaneously as Hilary began to plummet. Arms in a crisp white shirt and legs in blue denim shorts flailed wildly in the air as she plunged toward the hard wooden stage below.

Megan watched in horror as her best friend began to descend toward certain death.

And then, in the blink of an eye, one of Hilary's grasping hands came into contact with a rope dangling on her left.

The hand grabbed.

Clutched.

And held.

There was a moment of breathless silence as the three onlookers stood paralyzed with shock below their dangling friend.

Megan, with a little moan of relief, sank to her knees on the worn red carpeting. Hilary's life had nearly ended.

Like Juliet's had, so long ago.

"Help!" Hilary called weakly, her voice hoarse

with panic. "Get me down! Hurry! I can't hold on!"

The two boys ran for a ladder.

On shaky legs, Megan got up and hurried down the aisle, her gait as disjointed as a toddler's. She kept her eyes on Hilary as she climbed the wooden steps up to the stage. "Hang on, Hilary, don't let go," she urged. "They're bringing a ladder. Hang on!"

When Hilary, her face an unhealthy gray, her body shaking violently, had been rescued and was lying on the stage trying to catch her breath, Megan, kneeling beside her and holding Hilary's hand, asked, "What happened? Did you slip?"

Hilary shook her head. "Didn't. Didn't slip. Pushed."

"Pushed?" Megan sank back on her heels. The drawing. A definite warning.

Hilary couldn't stop shaking. Her arms and legs rapped against the wooden floor like the wings of a frightened bird. But anger quickly began to replace the panic. "Of course I was pushed. I certainly didn't jump. Ken Waters isn't *that* great." She looked up at her fellow crew members. "You guys see who it was?"

One had been busy sweeping up backstage, the other had been returning equipment to the prop room. And Megan had been too far back in the auditorium to see or hear anything.

"I don't like this at all," Megan said slowly, helping Hilary sit up. "If you hadn't grabbed that rope . . ."

"You probably fell, Bench," one of the boys said.

Hilary shuddered. Her blue eyes, still glazed with shock, glanced up toward the catwalk. "I did not fall," she said firmly as the boys helped her to her feet. "I am not a *falling* sort of person. Anyway, I know every inch of that catwalk as well as I know my own bedroom. Someone pushed me."

"Well, we didn't see anything," one of the boys repeated. "Boy, were you ever lucky! Talk about quick reflexes. You ever do any gymnastics, Bench?" There was awe and admiration in his voice.

"No. And I don't see how you can joke about this." Hilary bit her lower lip. "It's a long way down from up there." She closed her eyes briefly, another violent shudder shaking her body. "I'm reporting this to Mr. Shattuck."

"He'll just blow it off, Hil," the other boy said. "Nobody saw anything."

"I don't care. I *felt* it." Hilary bent carefully to pick up her books and purse from the floor. "You coming with me, Megan?"

Megan had planned to go home and seek out Juliet. But she couldn't leave a shaky Hilary.

Should she take the drawing to Mr. Shattuck? How could she? It was only a curved line on a piece of paper. It had been meant only for Megan. Whoever drew it knew she would understand. And she had. But Mr. Shattuck wouldn't.

"Of course I'm coming, Hilary. Here, let me carry your stuff." She reached for Hilary's things. "You're not going to pass out, are you?"

"No, I'm not going to pass out," Hilary said in a slightly steadier voice. "If I were a *passing-out* kind of person, I'd have done it when I was hanging from that rope like a piece of meat in a butcher shop. And I can carry my own things."

Megan felt relief wash over her. Hilary not only was not hurt, she was getting back to normal very quickly. She was a very lucky girl.

So was Megan. What would she ever do without Hilary?

As they made their way up the aisle, Hilary managed a weak smile. "I'm sorry I don't have a broken wing so you could feel sorry for me and fix me up, Megan. You're so good at that."

"Hil! I'm *glad* you're not hurt." Impulsively Megan turned to give Hilary a hug.

"Oh, Megan, I know you're glad. I was just teasing." Hilary paused, and then added, "Megan, you believe I was pushed, don't you? I mean, I wouldn't make up something like that."

Megan felt guilty about not sharing the drawing with Hilary. But Hil was already so shaken. Proof positive that she really had been a target would only upset her more.

"Of course I believe you."

"Well, don't you think it's scary? First there's Jenny's accident, which turns out not to be an accident at all, and now someone sends me off into space from the catwalk. Something really nasty is going on here."

Hilary continued to fume about the incident, but Megan wasn't listening. She was lost in her thoughts. Why would someone push Hilary? Push her, knowing that such a fall would kill her? And it had to be the same person who was drawing those pictures.

That meant someone at the school, someone who had access to the art room. Donny, rejected by so many girls? Vicki Deems, Viper Extraordinaire, who always had that cold, hungry look in her eyes? Was she viciously trying to destroy the competition, and keep all the boys for herself?

Megan and Hilary were both still very shaken when they arrived at the principal's office and told their story. But the boys had been right. Because no one had seen Hilary's attacker, Mr. Shattuck, a cautious man, chose to regard the incident as an "unfortunate accident." He then called Hilary's mother to come and take her home, being very careful not to alarm her.

While they waited in the hall for Mrs. Bench, Hilary said angrily, "He didn't believe me. So he won't have it investigated, and whoever pushed me will get away with it, just like he's getting away with the car tampering."

"He won't get away with it. The sheriff is still investigating, according to my mom."

Hilary shrugged.

"Are you sure you're okay?" Megan asked with concern. "Your face is the color of my old gym socks. And your eyes look glazed, like you're not really in there."

"I'm fine. I'm just mad now. Quit worrying. Let my mom do that. It's her job."

When Hilary had been deposited safely in her mother's very competent hands, Megan went to look for Justin. He had said he'd be in the *Scribe* office.

Walking down the hall, the sight of Hilary falling, falling, returned to Megan's mind, and she closed her eyes, feeling like she'd been riding on an out-of-control Ferris wheel. If Hilary hadn't caught that rope . . . Megan leaned against the wall until the nausea passed.

Why was all this happening? In the past two days *four* girls had narrowly escaped death. And every one of them was a good friend of Megan's.

Was she in danger, too? Was that why she felt shadowed? Because someone *was* watching her? Watching . . . and waiting . . .

Shaking her head to erase the image of Hilary's dreadful fall, Megan continued on down the hall.

The door to the *Scribe* office was open when she arrived. As she stepped inside, the tiny hairs on the back of her neck rose. Justin was seated at his desk as usual, a pencil nesting over one ear. But seated on his desk, not at all as usual, was Vicki Deems, a bright red halter top and a black leather miniskirt fitted snugly around her beautiful body. She was leaning forward, a curtain of silky black hair draping one tanned cheek. She seemed to be whispering in Justin's ear.

And what was worse, he seemed to be listening.

Megan froze in the doorway. What if she'd waited too long to ask Justin to be her date for the party? What if he asked Vicki? After all, Justin was a healthy, normal, red-blooded American male. And that was *some* halter top.

"Oh, hello, Megan," Vicki said in a husky voice that set Megan's teeth on edge.

Megan allowed herself the satisfaction of seeing Justin glance up guiltily, his gorgeous face flushing scarlet, before she turned and ran. Even when she heard him calling out her name, she kept going.

She ran all the way home in a vain effort to escape two awful images. One was of Hilary plunging toward the stage, a picture that sent Megan's stomach into sickening nausea. The other image was of Justin with his head next to Vicki's. That one filled her with fury.

When she was safe in her own room, in her own house, she grimly put all thoughts of friends in danger, vicious vipers, and treacherous males out of her head. She had more important things to think about.

Because ever since Hilary had grabbed that rope and hung on for dear life, ever since they'd put that ladder up there and a shaky but unharmed Hilary had slowly climbed down to safety, Megan had known that she was going to trade places with Juliet. She just hadn't been ready to admit it to herself. Until now.

The idea no longer seemed so crazy, so impossible. The way she felt now had something to do with four of her closest friends almost losing their lives but being lucky enough to survive. Luckier than Juliet. And all Juliet wanted was one tiny little week. That wasn't very much.

Her gratitude that Hilary's body hadn't crashed into that hard wooden stage made her feel generous.

Scared, *terrified* even, but generous. What was a week, anyway? Practically nothing.

Hadn't Gram said Megan marched to a different drummer? Maybe it was time to prove that. Something deep inside her, something she had never listened to before, was willing to do this incredibly frightening thing. It was time to pay attention to that part of her.

Dropping her books and purse on the bed, Megan took a deep breath and walked over to the mirror. "Juliet, are you there?" she called softly. "I want to talk to you."

The mirror remained clear. There was no plume of purplish haze, no faintly glowing silvery light, no whispering voice. There was nothing but glass and Megan's own reflection.

Chapter 8

When the mirror stared blankly back at her, Megan fought a mixture of relief and disappointment.

Where *was* Juliet?

Every five or ten minutes during the evening, Megan called out Juliet's name. But there was no answer.

After phoning Hilary to make sure she was really okay, Megan crawled into bed, but she wasn't planning on sleeping. She would stay awake and continue trying to summon Juliet.

But the horrors of the day had exhausted her. She fell asleep.

And was awakened during the night by a terrifying nightmare, the worst she'd ever had. A dense forest of cobwebs, soft and furry as caterpillars, imprisoned her. She struggled frantically to break free, but the steel-strong network refused to release her. Off in the distance, a giant spider approached slowly on thick, black, hairy legs.

Megan thrashed and moaned, desperately seeking freedom. But the web held.

Somewhere in the distance, she heard her name called softly. But she was powerless to answer.

Panicking halfway between sleep and wakefulness, she bolted upright in bed, suddenly wide awake. Stunned, she looked around her, but could see nothing in the pitch-black. The dream had been so real. She had felt so absolutely trapped. The feeling of helplessness stayed with her. Her stomach lurched, her head ached with a pain that hurt her eyes, and she was very, very cold.

And then she realized that the cold came from the now-familiar plunge in the room's temperature.

Megan shivered, desperately wanting the darkness to disappear. She could still feel the threat of that enormous hairy spider ambling toward her in the dream web. Shuddering again, she wrapped her arms around her chest and watched numbly as the mirror began to fill with the shimmering lavender image.

"I'm sorry I didn't come earlier," Juliet apologized. "I heard you calling me. But I was scared you'd decided not to trade, and I couldn't stand to hear you say it." Then, "Megan, what's wrong? You look awful!"

"I'm okay." Megan took a deep breath and exhaled. "Juliet, I've thought about it. I want you to explain again about trading."

The plume danced with amazement and joy. "You do?"

"Yes. Exactly how would we do it? Tell me everything."

"Oh, it's so easy!" Juliet's voice rose and fell with

excitement. "Once you agree, all you have to do is step into this mirror. And I will step out . . . as you. It takes only a second."

"And I will be invisible, but you will be able to hear me?"

"Yes. And nothing from your world can touch you."

"But . . . it can touch *you*. And you will be *me*. That scares me, Juliet. It means that whoever hurt my friends and pushed Hilary off the catwalk, could go after me . . . you . . . next. Are you *sure* you can protect yourself better than I could?"

"Yes, Megan, I am sure. I'll be careful."

Megan wished she could have talked to someone about all of this. But who would believe her? She hardly believed it herself.

Reading her thoughts, Juliet warned, "You can't tell anyone, Megan. I know it's hard, but that would ruin everything. The only one who can know is the lender, and that's you. No one else."

"You think you know enough about me to act and talk like me?" she asked Juliet.

"It's only for a week, Megan. I can handle that."

"And you will look just like me?"

"I will *be* you, Megan. I will look like you and talk exactly like you. But inside, I'll still be me. And you'll still be you. No one can take your real inner self from you."

Juliet's voice was calm and reassuring, as if they were discussing taking a walk around the lake.

Megan tried to relax. "We would have to practice switching before I agreed."

"Of course. There's nothing to it. You step into the mirror and I step out. As you."

She was right. There wasn't anything to it. After each transformation, Megan felt nothing but a peculiar sense of weightlessness, the way she imagined a soap bubble might feel. She disliked the dark emptiness of the mirror, but Juliet reminded her that there was no need for her to remain there.

"You can go anywhere you want, as long as you don't leave the lake area."

They switched back and forth four times without a hitch. The strangest part was looking out from inside the mirror and seeing her physical self, now Juliet, standing there before her. When Megan wanted to be herself again, she simply said, "I am Megan, and I want to be me again." And she was.

Her voice quivering with excitement, Juliet said after the fourth trial, "When can we do this, Megan? It has to be soon. There's hardly any time left before your birthday."

Megan made up her mind. She had thought about her friends, all nearly losing their lives so young, like Juliet. Narrow escapes had saved them. Juliet hadn't been so lucky. Juliet had this one chance to live again, for one tiny little week. It would be wrong not to let her have that. One week wasn't such a big deal.

And there was something else. If there was any chance at all that Juliet could somehow sense who was responsible for the pain and fear in Lakeside, Megan had to take that chance.

"I've already decided," Megan said quietly. "It

has to be tomorrow night. You'll have a full week, and we'll switch back again next Saturday night in time for my party on Sunday. I *have* to be at my party." Setting a definite time for the trade sent butterflies of fear fluttering around Megan's stomach. But she had made up her mind. She wouldn't go back on her word now.

Juliet shrieked with joy. "I can't believe it! At last! Oh, it's going to be so wonderful!" The plume began dancing in excitement. "I'm going to have a whole week!"

The shadows in the room lightened a bit. It was almost dawn. "It's today already," Megan murmured, her heart sounding a drumroll in her chest as she thought about what the evening would bring. "It's Saturday now."

Juliet moved happily in the mirror. "And you promise you won't change your mind, will you, Megan?"

Megan shook her head.

"Then I'll go now. I'm so excited! I hope the day passes quickly. Just call my name tonight when you're ready, and I'll be here. And Megan, thank you, thank you, thank you!"

As the mirror image faded, and the room brightened, Megan fought a wild desire to call Juliet back and tell her she'd changed her mind, that the whole idea was impossible. But she turned away from the mirror decisively. She'd given her promise.

Megan took an early shower and spent the day running errands in preparation for her party.

Hilary called to tell her that Jenny still wasn't

allowed visitors, and that there was no news from Sheriff Toomey. "I don't think he's even questioned anyone," she said, adding darkly, "*I* could give him the names of a couple of good suspects!"

Megan hung up, feeling traitorous. Here she was doing this incredibly strange, scary thing and she hadn't shared any of it with her best friend. But Juliet had made it clear that telling anyone would ruin everything.

Justin called twice, calls Megan didn't return. Let Juliet deal with him. Juliet would have to ask him to Megan's party, too, because it was the only thing left undone on the lists. There it was, in black and white: *ASK JUSTIN*.

Walking over to the mirror after dusk, her hands trembling, her knees like pudding, Megan called Juliet's name softly, wishing fiercely that she could have told her parents what she was doing. But of course she couldn't have. They would never understand. Never!

Before she and Juliet actually made the switch, Megan asked tentatively, "There's just one more thing, Juliet. I was wondering — "

Juliet interrupted her. "Yes, I'll ask Justin to your party. And he will say yes, don't worry."

Unable to think of a good reason to stall any longer, Megan nodded, took a deep breath, and stepped into the mirror.

Chapter 9

To Megan's distress, the sensations that came with the final transformation were very different from the practice switches. Instead of the lightness she'd felt before, there was a horrible wrenching sensation, as if steel arms were tugging and tearing at her.

And when those awful sensations passed, leaving her with no feeling at all, the blackness in which she found herself was unrelieved and icy cold. Beyond the darkness, she could see her room. But it seemed very far away, as if she were looking through a telescope.

Wild with fear, she cried out, *"Juliet! Juliet, are you there? I don't see you. Where are you?"*

And a girl who looked exactly like Megan Logan appeared in front of the mirror, a happy smile on her face. "I'm right here, Megan. I hear you. Relax!" Her voice and speech sounded exactly like Megan, too. "Remember, you can talk to me any time you want."

Her words failed to dilute the abject terror Megan felt. *What have I done?* she thought wildly. *"Juliet, I feel terrible. So far away from everything. It's not like it was when we practiced. Why does it feel so different now?"*

"It's because you're not practicing this time, Megan. But it's just a week. Anyway, you'll feel better soon. Don't worry."

Then, touching her cheeks, her hair, her arms with wonderment, Juliet said, "Oh, I can't believe this!" A radiant smile lifted her lips. "I'm going to have such a wonderful time!"

The seven days that had earlier seemed so brief to Megan now stretched ahead of her like a dark, endless tunnel. *This is horrible,* she thought miserably. *I feel like I've been sucked into a bottomless pit. I'll never be able to stand this for seven whole days!*

Only Juliet's obvious joy kept her from reneging on her promise. Megan forced herself to calm down, to tell herself that it would be all right.

She let herself be distracted by Juliet's excitement. *"You'd better chill out,"* she warned gently. *"I'm not a bouncing-off-the-walls person. People will be suspicious."*

"You're right. I'll try. But I'm so excited. And right now I'm off to the bathroom to take a wonderful bath and put on just a tiny bit more makeup. Then I'm off! This is Saturday night. I've got places to go, people to see."

Juliet paused in front of the mirror and said, "Megan, thank you! You won't be sorry."

But Megan was already sorry. And scared.

Before Megan could utter any one of the thousand new questions spinning around her, Juliet, with a happy wave and an equally happy smile, was out the door.

The thud it made as it closed felt to Megan like the closing of a tomb.

I'm overreacting. Being silly. I'll just get out of this dark, cold place, and everything will be fine, just like Juliet said.

But it wasn't. When she left the mirror, the sensation of darkness, of coldness, of being totally separated from the world she knew was devastating.

No one can see me. No one can hear me. As far as the world is concerned, I'm not here. Is this how Juliet felt all those years? So isolated? How lonely it feels not to be a part of the world!

The only way to ease the feeling was to go where there were people. There was no reason for her to stay in the bedroom, alone. So Megan went downstairs.

Her family was gathered in the kitchen. Megan remembered then that Thomas was in a play that night. He had the lead in a production of *Peter Pan* at Circle-in-the-Square Theater.

Although the loneliness Megan felt was eased somewhat by being around people, watching her family was like looking at one of those What's Wrong With This Picture? drawings.

I'm watching myself eat and laugh and talk . . . but it's not me. It's Juliet. And no one in this room knows that but the two of us. How can my parents not know? Can't they see that Juliet is laughing more and talking more than I do?

And then there was Juliet's makeup.

She looks like someone straight out of a forties movie. I never wear blue eyeshadow, and she must have at least eight coats of mascara on those eyes. I should have gone into the bathroom with her and helped her out.

"You're not wearing all that goop to my play, are you?" Thomas asked Juliet.

She stared at him. "Play? I'm not going to any play. I'm going to the mall."

Megan groaned silently.

"You're not going to the play?" Megan's mother echoed. "But we've planned this all week. I thought you and Justin had agreed to meet there. Isn't he doing a write-up on it for the school paper? And Hilary will be there, too. Betsy's in it, remember?"

Megan told Juliet, *"Betsy is Hilary's little sister, Juliet. We've been planning for weeks to go to this play tonight."* Talking and knowing only Juliet could hear her made her feel even more isolated.

Juliet laughed. "I was just kidding," she told the family quickly. "Of course I'm going to the play. I wouldn't miss it. It'll be fun."

"Well, good," Megan's mother said. "Because we definitely don't want you wandering around town by yourself. Not until Sheriff Toomey can tell us there's no risk involved. You'll be safe with us at the theater, and I won't have to worry."

While they finished eating, Megan wrestled with a strong desire to call off the whole thing. Watching Juliet being her was so much harder than she'd thought it would be. She had expected it to be like watching herself in one of her dad's homemade videos. But this wasn't anything like that. She always knew that was *her* on the television screen. No matter how silly or how stupid she felt, she always knew she was watching *herself* on tape.

But watching Juliet as Megan Logan made her feel the way she'd felt in the nightmare . . . trapped, imprisoned. And knowing that she couldn't reach out and touch her parents, touch Thomas, increased her sense of desolation.

How was she going to make it through a whole week of this?

Miserable, frightened, and more lonely than she had ever been, Megan followed her family to the Circle-in-the-Square Theater.

Chapter 10

The theater was air-conditioned and packed. Megan noticed that hers weren't the only parents accompanied by teenagers. Hilary had told everyone who would listen that she'd been pushed off the catwalk. Most of the parents had believed her. Fear shone from their eyes.

"What's with the war paint?" Hilary asked as she joined the Logan family in front-row seats. "Have you been sampling the goodies at Phar-Mart's cosmetics counter?"

Juliet laughed and shrugged. "I thought it was time for a change. I *am* going to be sixteen, Hilary. Have you seen Justin?"

"He's parking. He'll be here in a minute. So, did you ask His Royal Cuteness to be your birthday date yet?"

"I'm asking him tonight. And he'll say yes," Juliet answered.

Hilary looked impressed. "Wow! I guess it's true what the ads say about makeup. You *are* a new woman!"

Megan warned, *"Careful, Juliet. Don't overdo the 'new woman' bit or Hil will guess that you're not only a new me, you're not even a me at all."*

If Justin was surprised by the enthusiastic reception Juliet gave him when he arrived, he hid it well. At intermission in the lobby, she chattered, laughed at his quips, and held his hand the whole time.

Megan, watching miserably, reminded herself that Justin, after all, thought that it was Megan flirting with him. And he certainly seemed to be enjoying himself. But seeing Juliet having such a good time with him was hard to take. Megan wanted so much to touch Justin, the way Juliet was doing. And she couldn't. For one long, endless week she wouldn't be able to touch him or smile at him or talk to him.

Megan now realized that it was going to be the longest week she'd ever known.

After the play, Constance Logan insisted that everyone come back to the house, squelching Juliet's plans to be alone with Justin. "I know you think I'm a worrywart," Megan's mother said apologetically, "but I'd really feel better if you were at the house. Humor me, okay? Justin and Hilary can come along, too."

"But it's Saturday night!" Juliet protested. "Everyone will be at the mall."

Mrs. Logan shook her head. "I don't think so. I talked to a lot of the other parents tonight, and they're keeping their kids home, too." She patted a disconsolate Juliet on the shoulder. "It's just for a few days, honey, until Sheriff Toomey catches whoever tampered with those cars and pushed poor Hilary off that catwalk. I'm sure everything will be back to normal in time for your birthday party."

Juliet looked stricken. Her eyes widened and her face paled as she drew in a deep breath of dismay.

She's seeing her week of fun going down the tubes. I tried to tell her this was a lousy time in Lakeside. But I guess it was now or never. Poor Juliet.

When they got to the house, Thomas and his father took the boat out. Mrs. Logan went down on the dock to "relax and enjoy the night sky," and Justin talked Hilary and Juliet into watching a science-fiction movie in the den.

Since Justin seemed to be enjoying Juliet's company so much, Megan began to wonder if he would be disappointed when the week was up and the "old" Megan returned.

I could never be like her, all sparkly and giddy and outgoing. No wonder she was popular forty-five years ago. I couldn't be like that . . . could I?

Hilary, Megan noticed, didn't seem to be having very much fun, though. She looked almost as lost and lonely as Megan felt. And she kept looking at Juliet, obviously confused by her friend's un-Meganlike behavior.

Poor Hil can't understand why all of a sudden I'm Miss Personality. I wish I could have told her what was going on.

Megan decided to join her brother and her father

out on the lake. Maybe being out in the open would ease her misery.

The lake was crowded with boaters trying to escape the heat, including many of Megan's friends. She was happy to see Barbie Winn, a bandage across one side of her face, in a canoe with her boyfriend. She'd been luckier than her older sister. Donny Richardson went by in a boat crowded with people Megan guessed were relatives. The two boys who had rescued Hilary with the ladder went by, and so did Vicki Deems, surrounded by boys Megan didn't recognize. From a nearby town, probably. Vicki must have already conquered the entire male population of Lakeside and been forced to seek out fresh new territory.

Unfortunately Megan found that being outside with the trees and the lake around her did nothing to help her mood. Neither did venturing into the depths of the lake, where she discovered the cold and the wet couldn't touch her. Frustrated and unhappy, she surfaced, only to be again surrounded by laughter and chatter from the boats on the lake.

I would rather feel the wet and the cold than this terrible, empty feeling. Nothing could be worse than this. Nothing!

When her father aimed the boat toward home, Megan went, too.

As they neared the dock, something moving in the water caught her attention. Megan moved in closer to get a better look. What was it?

A tree branch? Remnants of someone's lakeside picnic?

Megan saw hair, splayed like seaweed on the water. She saw two arms, two legs. . . .

A voiceless scream soared up through her.

Her mother was floating, facedown and unconscious on the water.

Chapter 11

The sight of her mother's limp form floating like debris on the black water made Megan feel as helpless as she'd felt in the spiderweb dream. *I've got no voice, so I can't scream. I've got no body, so I can't drag her out of the water. And if she dies, it'll be all my fault. If I hadn't traded places with Juliet, I could save Mom now.*

Thomas's frantic shout broke through Megan's frustration. In a second, he was out of the boat and plunging through the shallow water to Constance Logan, crying out to his father. He grabbed at her shirt, ballooning out around her, full of air and water. His frantic shouting, "Mom, Mom!" was high and shrill with fear. His father arrived at his side, and together they lifted the unconscious woman and carried her up the embankment.

Megan wanted, needed, desperately to help her family. There was only one way she could do that. She raced up to the house. *Mom, Mom, please don't be dead!*

Inside the house, she sought out the only person

who could hear her cry for help. She found Juliet in the den with Justin. They were seated, very close together, on the velvet settee. Hilary was nowhere in sight.

"*Juliet! Juliet, quick! Dial nine-one-one! It's Mom! In the lake. Hurt. Hurry! I'll tell you what to say.*"

Juliet flew off the settee and rushed to the telephone on the table beside the bookshelves. At that moment, Thomas ran into the room, crying. He repeated the chilling news. In his panic, he failed to notice that Juliet had already dialed Emergency Services and was beginning to repeat the words Megan fed her.

"Dad's doing CPR on her right now," Thomas told Justin. "But she's . . . she hasn't moved."

As Juliet hung up the phone, Thomas turned to her. "I'm scared. She isn't even *moving*."

"Let's go!" Justin urged.

"Emergency Services will be here right away," Juliet said as they ran out of the house and down the slope. "I told them to come straight down to the dock."

"Do you have a crystal ball you haven't told me about?" Justin asked Juliet as they raced through the darkness.

"What?" Juliet asked.

"You had already gone to the phone *before* Thomas came in. How did you know something was wrong?"

"Oh," Juliet said, startled. "I saw them. Through the den window. I knew something was wrong."

Apparently satisfied with that explanation, Justin nodded and increased his speed.

When they reached the dock, Megan's mother was half sitting, half lying against her husband's chest. Although she was choking and coughing and gasping for breath, they were all relieved to see that she was conscious.

A siren in the distance announced the approaching ambulance.

"You okay, Mom?" Thomas asked, kneeling at his mother's side. "What happened? You're a good swimmer."

"I wasn't swimming," she answered weakly. "I was sitting. On the dock. Just thinking, enjoying all of the lights out on the water. And . . . and something hard hit me from behind. That's all I remember." She tried to smile. "Like they say in the movies, everything went black." She moved one hand to the back of her head, and when she brought it back down, the light from the boat lantern shone on a red, sticky mess.

With a dying shriek, the ambulance arrived. Megan's father rode with it to the Medical Center. He asked Justin to follow with Juliet and Thomas.

Megan, too, went in the ambulance. While the attendants cared for her mother, she fought rising panic. First, her closest friends had been attacked, nearly killed. Now someone had deliberately hit her mother on the head and watched as she fell into the lake, leaving her to drown.

But who? Everyone liked Megan's mother. Like the other victims, she had no enemies. Until now.

We have to switch back. Now! I hate to go back on my promise and disappoint Juliet, but I can't just stand by and watch while some maniac hurts my family. I hope Juliet understands. I never should have agreed to switch in the first place.

When Constance Logan had been comfortably installed in a hospital bed, a thick white bandage on the back of her head, her husband announced that he was staying with her all night.

"No!" she cried, her eyes, clouded with medication, snapping open with alarm. "I want you home with the children. I don't want them in the house alone, not now!"

"Yes, I suppose you're right," Tom Logan agreed, and he took his family home.

When Juliet had told Justin good night and gone upstairs, Megan followed.

"Juliet, I'm scared. Seeing my mother lying there in the water made me realize how helpless I am like this. I mean, I couldn't pull her out, and I couldn't scream. It was really terrible. I don't ever want to feel like that again. We have to switch back. Now!"

Juliet, searching through Megan's denim shoulder bag, scattering papers and old tissues every which way on the bed, had just located the hairbrush she'd been seeking and had begun to brush the dark curls absentmindedly. At Megan's words, she dropped the brush, her eyes filling with tears. "Oh, no, Megan, you can't mean that!" she cried. "You can't! I haven't even had a whole day yet!"

Megan felt like she was yanking the wings off a butterfly. *"I know. And I'm sorry, Juliet, I really am. I know I promised you a whole week. But I didn't expect anything like this to happen. Not being able to help my mother, Juliet, it was . . . it was horrible!"*

To her dismay, Juliet burst into tears. Between sobs, she begged, "Megan, please, please, don't do this! Your mother's going to be fine, the doctor said so. This means so much to me! It's the only chance I'll ever have. I'll help take care of your mother for you, I promise!"

Oh, God, I want this to end now, Megan thought even as Juliet's pleas tore at her resolve. She had never seen anyone so desperate. *"Juliet, it's just such a bad time — "* she began weakly.

Juliet interrupted with fresh tears. "Megan, I told you," she gasped, "there *isn't* any other time for me!" Skinny rivulets of mascara streaked her face. "Any other time will be too late for me." Her voice fell to a heartbroken whisper. "Too late, too late . . ."

The last ounce of Megan's resolve disintegrated in the face of Juliet's anguish. She had never in her life caused anyone so much pain, and she couldn't stand it. *"All right,"* she said with a helpless sigh, *"we won't switch back tonight. Now stop crying, okay?"*

Juliet lifted her head, her face filled with hope. "You mean it?"

"I . . . I guess so. We'll give it a little more time. But if anything else bad happens, Juliet, to my family or my friends, we're trading back."

"Of course, Megan." Wiping her tearstained face

with a towel, Juliet smiled and nodded. "But no more bad things are going to happen. I can feel it. Everything's going to be fine." Happy again, she slipped into Megan's white pajamas and climbed into the canopied bed. "If we hadn't switched," she said calmly, "you wouldn't have been down on the dock to find your mother and rush up to the house to call for help. So it's not all bad, is it, Megan? Being me, I mean?"

She had a point. But Megan wasn't consoled. The days and nights loaned to Juliet felt like years, centuries. On this, only the first night, they stretched ahead of her like an endless, dark, deserted highway. How would she ever get through them?

"Oh, by the way, Megan," Juliet said cheerfully as she pulled the sheet over her legs, "when Hilary left, I asked Justin to your party. And he said yes. So now you can quit worrying." She slid down in bed and closed her eyes. "Everything's going to be great. Your mom will be fine, and Justin is coming to your party. So relax, okay?"

"Juliet, what happened to Hilary tonight? Why did she go home so early?"

"Oh, I guess she felt like a third wheel. Good night, Megan. See you tomorrow."

A minute later, the sound of her deep, even breathing told Megan that Juliet was sound asleep. Just then, something on the worn blue carpet beside the bed caught Megan's eye. She knew what it was immediately, and the realization sickened her. How could another drawing have found its way into her home?

She knew she had to look at it. Otherwise it would lie there all night like some dreadful insect, tormenting her.

The picture was on lime-green paper. There were two crude crayon drawings. One was of a man in a gray-and-black-striped uniform. A convict. The second drawing was of a leg, awkwardly bent to emphasize the knee. CON. KNEE. Connie. Mom.

She remembered Juliet pulling things out of her shoulder bag. The drawing must have been in there. But how had it got there?

The mall. Someone had to have slipped it into her purse while she was there. If she hadn't been so distracted all day by the thought of what was ahead of her that evening, she would have noticed the drawing sooner. Then she could have done something, anything, to protect her mother. She could at least have warned Juliet not to leave her mother alone for a second.

At least her mother was alive. And she was going to be okay. She'd be home tomorrow, safe and sound.

But . . . it might not be over. What if there was another attack, this time on Juliet? Juliet had said she could prevent that. What if she couldn't? Maybe she was wrong.

If she was . . . if something happened to prevent their trade on Saturday night, something that kept Megan from returning to her own body . . . what would become of Megan?

Megan had to know, and she had to know *now.* "*Juliet! Wake up, Juliet! I have to talk to you.*"

"What . . ." a sleepy Juliet mumbled from bed. "What is it, Megan?"

"There's one thing you haven't told me, and I must know. What would happen to me . . . if you were . . . if something happens to my body while you're in it? I need to know that, Juliet."

"If something happened to stop you from returning to your own form by midnight Saturday," Juliet said slowly, "you'd . . . you'd be trapped in my world."

Megan gasped. *"And you weren't even going to tell me, were you?"*

"I didn't want to frighten you, Megan. Because nothing bad can happen to me. I can steer clear of evil better than you can. Your body is safer with me than it would be with you."

Megan heard none of what Juliet was saying. All she could think of was being trapped in this horrible, empty world . . . forever. It was too terrifying to comprehend.

Megan went out on the terrace roof to try to fathom what Juliet had just told her. Everything was perfectly still. Not a single leaf on the oak tree stirred. The lake was quiet, lying between the two shores like a giant ink stain. One by one, the lights in the houses bordering the lake went out, until, with no moon visible in the pouting gray sky, the darkness was complete.

Megan had never felt so alone in her life.

Chapter 12

Residents of Lakeside were severely shaken by the attack on Connie Logan. There was talk of hiring a private security patrol for the area. But the proposal was voted down because of the expense.

Megan called Juliet's attention to the drawings. *"Keep your eyes open for more of these,"* she said. *"If someone else is going to get hurt, you might get another one. Check the art cubbyhole every day and the mailbox here at the house. And Juliet,"* she warned, *"I think Mom is right. I don't think it's a good idea to go out alone. It might not be safe."*

Juliet didn't argue. She didn't want to be alone, anyway. She wanted Justin with her, preferably at all times. "I know he's your boyfriend," she told Megan happily, "but it's okay because he thinks I'm *you*. So it's not like I'm doing anything wrong, right, Megan?"

She didn't seem to be taking the drawings seriously. That bothered Megan. How was she going to keep watch over Juliet *and* her family, too?

Megan wished she could feel as confident about

Juliet's safety as Juliet seemed to. If there was a list of potential victims somewhere, Megan's name was surely on it. Everyone who had been hurt was close to her. If *she* could be next, that meant *Juliet* could be next.

She couldn't forget Juliet's answer to her question the night before. *"Juliet,"* she said as Juliet checked out the clothes in Megan's closet, *"I wish you'd pay more attention to what's going on in town. You don't seem to care at all. But if something happens to you . . ."*

Juliet selected several outfits and carried them to the bed. Spreading them out like food on a picnic table, she said nonchalantly, "Goodness, Megan, nothing's going to happen to me! I told you, I'll know if something evil comes near me."

But that wasn't good enough. It was making her crazy. *"But if something* does *happen . . . I'd have to stay . . . like this . . . forever?"*

"The same thing would happen to you that will happen to me, come midnight on Saturday. I'll disappear, poof!" She smiled happily. "But it'll be okay now, because you gave me this week. Stop worrying. Nothing's going to happen to me before Saturday."

Poof? She would go poof? And disappear? Forever? The sharp-toothed edges of Megan's trap closed around her. She could only pray that the hours and the days would fly by quickly.

And that Juliet was right about being able to protect herself.

* * *

Megan's father brought his wife home from the hospital at noon. While she slept, he gave Juliet permission to go to the library with Justin. Reluctant at first to have any family member leave the house, he relented when Juliet pointed out that she had a report due in social studies.

"Nobody is going to attack me in the library, Daddy," Juliet pleaded. "Besides, Justin will be with me."

He gave in then, and Juliet ran happily upstairs to change her clothes.

But Megan wasn't so sure the library was perfectly safe. The auditorium at Philippa should have been perfectly safe, too. But it hadn't been for Hilary, had it? Maybe no place in Lakeside was safe. And if Juliet and Justin got lost in each other the way they had the night before, an army of attackers could surround them and they wouldn't notice until it was too late.

By the time Justin arrived, Juliet, in a full white skirt and a silky red long-sleeved blouse and red sandals, was waiting at the front door. Her makeup was still slightly exaggerated, but she looked very pretty.

The look on Justin's face as Juliet came down the stairs depressed Megan. Would he wear that same expression when she was herself again?

When Justin had learned from Mr. Logan that Megan's mother was okay and sleeping comfortably, he and Juliet left, hand in hand.

Megan left, too. The only advantage to this horrible feeling of separation from the world was her ability to watch and listen without being seen or heard. She might as well use it. But it didn't take her long to realize that she wasn't going to learn anything on a dismal, cool Sunday afternoon in a village whose residents were too scared to venture from their homes.

The town was virtually deserted. A damp gray mist fell steadily on a lake empty of boats, on streets bare of automobiles and bicycles, on lawns free of children and pets, on deserted tennis courts and pools. Curtains and blinds were drawn on every house, gates closed and locked, garage doors firmly latched.

And Megan had no idea what to look for. A stranger with maniacal eyes skulking through backyards seeking out victims? Or someone familiar who *seemed* no different — but on the inside was sick and twisted?

It had to be someone she knew, someone who knew *her*. Someone who knew which art cubbyhole was hers, since there were no names on the boxes, someone who knew that denim shoulder bag belonged to her.

All kinds of people had been in the lake area last night. Which one of them had attacked her mother? And who did they intend to attack next?

Vicki Deems had been out on the lake. But if Vicki wanted Justin Carr for herself, how would hurting Connie Logan help her get him?

Maybe Vicki just hates everyone in Lakeside. That was a scary thought. But, picturing Vicki's cold, dark eyes, Megan found it easy to believe that the girl could hate someone enough to hurt them.

Discouraged because there was nothing to see or hear, Megan explored the lake for a while, then moved through the cool gray mist toward home.

She arrived to find Justin's red car parked in the driveway, facing the lake. That was no surprise. What was a surprise was finding Juliet and Justin still in it, seated so close together they looked like one person.

And they were kissing. Intensely.

Justin had kissed Megan before. But never like that. It had been more of an I-like-you-Megan-and-I'm-glad-we-know-each-other kind of kiss. Not a Wow-are-you-ever-terrific kind of kiss, which was what he was giving Juliet this very minute.

It was so hard to remember that Justin believed he was with *her*, Megan. She wanted so much to tell him the truth, to shout, "Justin, it's me, Megan, over here. That's not me you're kissing, it's a ghost named Juliet!"

But he wouldn't be able to hear her.

Justin pulled Juliet even closer. Mist clouded the windshield and the windows, obliterating the outside world. The pair didn't seem to mind.

Megan fled.

Twenty agonizingly long minutes later, when Juliet entered the bedroom, a dreamy smile on her face, Megan was waiting for her.

"*Juliet*," Megan said, "*someone could have come up behind that car and pushed it straight into the lake, and you and Justin wouldn't have known it until your shoes started to get soggy. I don't call that being careful!"*

Juliet threw herself across the unmade bed, rolled over on her back, and thrust a lace-edged pillow under her head. "Sounds to me like somebody's jealous," she said with a grin. "Gosh, Megan, I don't see why. Justin thinks that was *you* he was kissing." Another grin. "And kissing and kissing and . . . listen, I was doing you a big favor. Jump starting his motor for you."

"Justin's going to get suspicious. He knows I'm not that . . . that outgoing."

Juliet grinned, catlike. "He doesn't seem to mind."

Just then the phone rang.

"Oh, hello, Hilary." Juliet's voice became ice cream, smooth and cold. "Yes, my mother's fine. She came home this afternoon." She listened for a moment and then said, "Well, I just don't think I have anything to apologize for. You're too sensitive, that's all."

There was an audible click on the other end.

Juliet shrugged and replaced the phone.

Megan had been listening. *"What did you do to Hilary? Why does she want an apology?"*

"Because she's silly, that's why. And because she never learned that three is a crowd. My goodness, Megan, I learned that when I was two years old."

Megan, thinking that the last thing in the world Hilary needed right now was to have her feelings hurt, said, *"She didn't really leave last night be-*

cause she was tired, did she? Juliet, what did you do?"

The heat wave had finally broken, and a gust of wind sent a cool mist into the room, stirring the curtains. Juliet jumped up to close the window and then went to the closet and grabbed a white terrycloth robe hanging on the back of the door. "I simply said that it was too bad she didn't have a date on Saturday night and had to hang around with Justin and me. The next thing I knew, she was calling her father to come and pick her up, and five minutes later she was out of here. It's really not my fault, Megan. I didn't mean to hurt her feelings, but I wanted to be alone with Justin."

"You told her she was in the way? Juliet, that's awful!"

"I didn't hear Justin complaining." Her eyes became cloudy with pleasure. "Megan, if I'm going to make the most of this week, I can't do it with Hilary hanging over my shoulder."

And without waiting to hear any more, Juliet left to take a bath.

Megan stared longingly at the telephone. *If only I could pick it up and fix things with Hilary. She must be so down right now. How am I ever going to make this up to her?*

But there was nothing Megan could do, except wait. Six more days. Six *long* days.

Chapter 13

It became very clear to Megan the next morning that Juliet wasn't going to be much help to a recuperating mother, in spite of her promise to Megan to "take care of your mother."

"Dishes? Gosh, I don't have *time*! Justin's picking me up in two minutes. Can't Thomas do them?"

Thomas, gulping down the last of his cereal, howled a protest. "I have to put air in my bike tires. I don't have time for dishes."

Megan, watching, disapproved of both Juliet's attitude and her outfit. The perfectly innocent white peasant blouse Megan was so fond of looked very different on Juliet, who had pushed the tiny, puffed sleeves off her shoulders, baring them.

"I don't wear it like that," she had told Juliet upstairs.

"It's more fun like this," had been Juliet's response.

Hearing that her father had decided to take the day off to stay with his wife, Megan followed Juliet to school. Leaving Juliet alone for any length of time would be not only dangerous, but foolish. After Juliet had left, Megan heard her father turn to Thomas and say in a perplexed voice, "Now, what's got into that girl? She didn't even tell your mother good-bye."

Megan hoped that Juliet's behavior at school wouldn't cause the same reaction from her friends and teachers. Would everyone be chorusing, "What's got into Megan?" by the end of this week? Maybe even by the end of this day?

But none of that mattered as much as being sure that Juliet was safe. *Maybe my being around her won't protect her, but if I don't know that she's okay, I'll go crazy worrying.*

Fighting her anxiety, Megan searched the halls and classrooms at Philippa Moore for Juliet. The complete silence in the building seemed to Megan positively freakish. There was no laughter, no chatter, no footsteps clattering down the halls, no slamming of locker doors. The building itself seemed to be holding its breath, waiting to see where disaster would strike next.

Being in the school but separated from it by the hideous invisible wall between her and her familiar world made Megan wish ferociously that she hadn't daydreamed her way through so many classes. *I took it all for granted,* she scolded herself, *and now, if anything happens to Juliet, I might never get it back.*

No. That couldn't happen. It couldn't!

Megan found Juliet in the cafeteria with Hilary.

But her relief was short-lived when she realized they were arguing.

Juliet and Hilary were sitting at a corner table in the sparsely occupied room. Hilary's face was scarlet, her short, squat body rigid with anger. Juliet seemed perfectly relaxed.

Uh-oh. What's going on?

"You could at least say you're sorry!" Hilary said. "You embarrassed me in front of Justin. That stinks, Megan! I could have had a date Saturday night if I'd wanted one, and you know it."

Toying with a plastic fork on her tray, Juliet said, "Then why didn't you? I mean, Hil, you keep telling me to go for it with Justin. How do you expect me to do that with a chaperone around all the time?"

Hilary's mortified flush was painful for Megan to see. "Oh." Hilary's voice sank to a near-whisper. "I guess . . . I guess you're right. I'm sorry. I wasn't thinking. I didn't realize I was in the way."

Why isn't she fighting back? Hilary always fights back. She doesn't sound like herself any more than Juliet sounds like me.

Megan realized then that Hilary's plunge toward death had affected her far more deeply than she'd let anyone know.

Jenny and Cappie and I always knew that as tough as Hil was on the outside, she was a soft, warm marshmallow inside. She would die before she'd hurt anyone on purpose. And the idea that someone would deliberately hurt her, for no reason, has really shaken her.

And Juliet, whether she knew it or not, was making it worse.

Hilary stood up, clutching her books to her chest as if they might somehow protect her. "See you," she whispered, and hurried out of the cafeteria.

As angry as Megan was, she decided it would be foolish to confront Juliet here in the cafeteria. Juliet could hardly sit in a public place and reply to an unseen Megan's questions. She'd look like an idiot, talking to herself. Megan would have to wait until they were both back home.

As Juliet got up and left, Megan noticed that she was not the only person watching. Vicki Deems, seated alone off to Megan's right, had fixed her eyes on Juliet. They smouldered with . . . was that hatred? Why? Because Vicki wanted Justin?

If Vicki was evil enough to have hurt so many people, would Juliet be able to *feel* that when she shared an English classroom with Vicki later that day?

Before she left school, Megan went with trepidation to the art room. Approaching the cubbyhole cautiously, she said a quick prayer that it would be empty.

It wasn't.

The sheet of paper was a bright sunny yellow. It took her a few moments to decipher the message drawn in vivid purple. The crude strokes depicted what looked like a drum. A round, squat drum with a green zigzag trim bordering the top and bottom edges. Two short, skinny drumsticks with padded ends lay crisscross on top of the drum.

It's not a drum. It's a tom-tom. Thomas. Tom. There are two of them in my family: Big Tom and little Tom.

Was this drawing a threat to both of them? Her brother *and* her father?

Megan's cold and lonely world began spinning wildly around her. The tomblike silence of the building shouted at her, "Watch out for your family, Megan!"

Why hadn't Juliet told her about the drawing?

"I didn't go to art," was the answer Megan got when, at home, she asked that question. "Justin had to go pick up some stuff for *The Scribe,* so I cut and went with him. I hope you're not mad. I mean, nobody seems to think anything of it. Gosh, if I'd ever cut a class, my father would have killed me!"

"Not your mother?"

"My mother died when I was nine."

"Oh, I'm sorry, Juliet." What terrible things had happened to Juliet. First her mother's death, and then her own. And all she wanted now was this one week.

Still, Megan wished with all her heart that she had never given the week away. She wanted it back. But how could she do that to Juliet? It would be so cruel.

"Juliet, did you cut English, too?" Like art, English was an afternoon class. She shared it with Vicki.

"Yes. But I promise I won't do it again. I wouldn't want your teachers to be mad at you because of me."

Megan was bitterly disappointed. She had counted on Juliet to let her know if she sensed anything evil from Vicki. But she didn't want to say anything that might influence Juliet's reaction to Vicki. It would just have to wait.

As would another evening of fun for Juliet, as she discovered at dinner when Megan's father put his foot down.

"You're staying in tonight," he said emphatically as they finished their meal. Juliet had asked permission to meet Justin at Lickety-Split, the ice-cream store in the mall. "No one in this family is stepping one foot outside this house. Do I make myself clear?"

He looked tired. Worry lines etched a pattern across his forehead, and his thick white hair stuck up all over, a sure sign that he'd been nervously running his fingers through it.

What happened to Mom has really upset him. Poor dad. Then she remembered the new drawing. *If only there was some way I could warn him and Thomas.*

This time, Juliet didn't argue. She seemed to understand that arguing would get her nowhere. Although she pouted over the change in plans, she did the dishes and swept the kitchen floor before going upstairs.

Megan expected her to call Justin immediately to cancel their date, but she didn't. Instead, she took a shower, changed into jeans and a pretty green blouse, blew her hair dry, applied fresh makeup, and then sat down on the bed, a paperback novel in hand.

And stayed there until she heard Thomas go into his room and close the door, and shortly after that, the plodding footsteps of a very weary Tom Logan on the stairs. A minute later, the door to the master bedroom clicked shut.

And Juliet, with a whispered but triumphant, "Yes, yes, yes!" picked up the denim purse, tiptoed down the stairs, and out of the house. Megan knew she was on her way to Lickety-Split to meet Justin as planned.

Her disobeying Megan's father was more than annoying to Megan. It was frightening. Going out at night now was a risky, stupid thing to do. Juliet's need to have fun this week was easy to understand, but Megan couldn't just let her go. Anything could happen to her. And anything that happened to her happened to Megan, too.

The only solution was to go to the mall and make Juliet come back home before anyone knew she was gone.

Thinking again of the new drawing, Megan made sure that both her brother and her father were safe in their own beds.

Then she followed Juliet.

Chapter 14

Megan arrived at the mall to find Hilary arguing vehemently with Vicki Deems in the corridor outside of the ice-cream store. Justin and Juliet were inside, sitting opposite each other in one of the pink-and-white-striped booths. They were the only customers in the store, and they seemed blissfully unaware of the argument going on outside.

"Talk about the pot calling the kettle black!" Hilary shouted. Her voice echoed with a hollow ring amid the potted trees and park benches. Except for her and Vicki, the corridor was deserted. It was late. The only store open was Lickety-Split, which kept longer hours to attract the after-movie crowd. "You've got a lot of nerve calling Megan a flirt. Your own Flirt Alert is on attack status twenty-four hours a day, Deems. A living, breathing male passes within fifty feet of you and you're all over him like jelly on peanut butter!"

Megan felt a warm rush of affection for Hilary. Juliet had hurt her feelings, yet here was Hilary defending her.

"At least I'm not a hypocrite," Vicki fumed, her mouth twisted in contempt. "Little Miss Muffet in there pretended to be so sticky-sweet until she caught me talking to Justin. Then she bared her fangs."

"You never stood a chance with him. He's only interested in Megan. Give it up, Vicki. Get a life!"

Vicki's face went white with rage. "I don't *give* up. Ever. If Megan hadn't come into the *Scribe* office that day, Justin would have asked me to her party. I'm never wrong about things like that."

"In your dreams, Deems."

Enraged, but aware that Hilary wasn't going to back down, Vicki turned on her heels and stalked away. Her long, dark hair swayed on her shoulders like a black silk cape.

Megan wished fiercely that she could hug Hilary to thank her. She wouldn't have blamed her best friend if she'd agreed with Vicki, after the way Juliet had hurt her.

She'd never seen Vicki so angry. Did she really want Justin that much? And how far would she go to get him?

Inside the restaurant, Hilary refused to acknowledge the existence of Justin and Juliet. Head up, shoulders squared, she marched straight to the counter, where she ordered a half gallon of Triple Trouble ice cream. Then she waited, her back resolutely to the couple.

"Hil?" Justin called. "Come on over. You're not still mad, are you?"

Hilary half turned. "I wouldn't dream of intruding," she said stiffly. "I'm just here to pick up dessert. Ignore me. That shouldn't be a problem for you."

Justin got up then and came over to the counter. Draping an arm around Hilary's stiffened shoulders, he said, "Come on, Hil, ease up. We didn't mean to hurt your feelings the other night. We feel bad about it."

Hilary glanced over at Juliet. She was chewing on a straw and smiling at Justin. Her smile excluded Hilary.

"Yeah, I can see she's all broken up about it."

"Look," Justin said, "tell you what. I'll ask Megan's father if we can take his boat out. The weather stinks, but it'll be fun, anyway. Come on, Hil. You can't stay mad forever."

A strangled sound from behind them made them both turn around. Juliet, in the booth, sat up straight and rigid as a pole, her face muscles contracted in fear. "Boat?" she choked. "Justin, you didn't say anything to me about going out in a boat. I won't go!"

Megan was watching. *Poor Juliet. Look at her face. She's terrified of the lake because that's where she died. But they're not going to understand. They think she's me, and I would never react that way to a boat ride. They know I love the lake.*

But Hilary was no longer surprised by anything her best friend did. "Look," she said while an amazed Justin stared at Juliet. "I just came to get dessert, that's all. I had to promise my parents I'd be back in fifteen minutes. If I'm not, they're sending the militia after me. They're totally paranoid right now."

She paid for the ice cream and left without saying a word to Juliet, who didn't seem to notice.

Justin hurried over to the booth. "What was that all about?" he asked Juliet, peering into her face. "Since when aren't you ready and willing to take a boat ride?"

And Juliet, reaching out to grasp Justin's hands in her own, leaned across the table and said sadly, "Since my mother ended up floating in the lake. That really upset me."

That excuse made sense to Justin. Megan could tell that he had accepted it by the understanding look on his face.

"Oh. Yeah, sure. But you'll get over it, right?" Justin wasn't a great swimmer, but he loved boating.

"Sure. Of course. Now, let's talk about something else."

"What did you decide to do about the drawing you showed me?" Justin asked Juliet. "You planning to take it to Toomey?"

It took Juliet a moment to shift gears. "Drawing?"

"Yeah, you know. The one of Jenny's car."

It's a good thing I showed it to her, or she wouldn't have the faintest idea what Justin was talking about.

"Oh, right." Juliet shook her head. "I don't think he'd pay that much attention. It's just a drawing. Someone with a sick sense of humor could have drawn it. It's not proof of anything."

Justin doesn't know about the other two draw-ings. I never had the chance to tell him. But Juliet does. Why isn't she telling him?

When Justin went to pay the bill, Megan finally had a chance to speak to Juliet. *"Juliet, you have to get back home before Dad notices you're gone."* Juliet jerked upright with surprise when Megan spoke to her. *"If he gets mad enough, he'll cancel the party. And it's not safe out here, anyway."*

As the words registered, Juliet's heavily mas-caraed lashes fluttered with alarm. "Cancel? He can't do that."

"Yes he can. You'd better go home, now."

Immediately contrite, Juliet whispered, "I'll go right now Megan. I couldn't stand it if your party was canceled." She sighed heavily. "I guess I've been a real pain. I'm sorry. I'll try to shape up, I promise." She waved a hand in dismissal. "Now go away, quick, before Justin gets back."

Justin arrived, saying with a grin, "Talking to yourself, are you? They say that's the first sign of old age."

Megan stayed just long enough to witness Juliet gifting him with a brilliant smile. Then she went home, where she checked on her sleeping family and waited anxiously for Juliet's return. They had things to talk about.

To Megan's great relief, Juliet managed to get back into the house without waking either parent.

"Whew!" Juliet exclaimed when she entered the

bedroom and realized that Megan was present. "I made it! See, Megan? Nothing terrible happened. Your father doesn't even know I was gone."

Megan wasn't interested in talking about Juliet's little escapade. *"Why didn't you tell Justin about the other drawings? If he knew there were three, I think he'd agree that you should take them to Sheriff Toomey."*

"Oh, Megan, they're just *pictures.* The sheriff would think I was crazy if I came waltzing into his office with a bunch of crayon drawings. Anyway," she added with a shrug, "I don't want to spend my time with Justin talking about creepy stuff like that. It's not very romantic."

"You promised you'd help."

"And I will, Megan. I'll pay strict attention to everyone I meet tomorrow. If I sense anything from anyone, I'll tell you about it, I promise. Okay?"

"Juliet, listen, you have to be more careful," Megan said. *"I'm not talking about upsetting my best friend and cutting classes. I'm talking about taking so many chances with your . . . my . . . safety. You've got to be more careful. Can't you see how important it is?"*

Juliet sighed and nodded. "You're right, Megan. I guess I was just so excited, I . . . I freaked out. It's not a very good way to pay back a favor. I'm sorry. I'll be more careful, I promise."

"Thank you." Megan drifted toward the window, intending to go outside, when she spotted a small white card on the dresser. According to its bright blue printing, Megan Logan had a hair appointment

at Cut It Again, Sam, a hair salon in the mall, on Saturday afternoon at one o'clock.

"Juliet, what is this? I don't have a hair appointment."

Juliet looked up from the bed in dismay. "Oh, Megan, it was supposed to be a surprise! You forgot to put it on your list, so I made the appointment for you."

"But I don't want to have my hair done."

Light laughter. "Of course you do. Megan, you can't go to your Sweet Sixteen party with" — she lifted a hand and gave a black curl a careless toss — "this."

"Yes, I can. I like my hair the way it is," Megan said. *"Just don't make plans without asking me first, okay? And cancel the hair appointment."*

Visibly disappointed, Juliet agreed to cancel the appointment. "I can't do it tonight. I'll do it tomorrow. But I still think your hair should look special for your Sweet Sixteen party, Megan. I wouldn't have dreamed of not going to the beauty parlor before my party."

"Well, you're not me, are you?"

That struck Juliet as being very funny, since, for the moment, she *was* Megan. She was still laughing to herself when she went to brush her teeth.

Megan hadn't found it that funny.

When Juliet had fallen asleep, Megan went outside. The lake and the surrounding area looked deceptively peaceful.

How am I going to keep an eye on Juliet and on Thomas and Dad? Even in this form, I can't be in three different places at the same time. But any one of them could be attacked at any time.

The thought of anything bad happening to her father or brother sickened Megan.

But a threat to Juliet was even more terrifying.

What do I do if something happens to my body and I can't return to it? Oh, God, I can't think about that. I won't!

But the question wouldn't go away. It pounded at her relentlessly, slapping at her, demanding to be answered. What would she do if something interfered with the exchange Saturday night?

She found no answer in the thick gray mist. Or in the night sky, black as coal. No answer in the smooth, glassy surface of the lake.

There was no answer anywhere.

Chapter 15

For the next two days, Megan stayed close to Juliet. She had decided, after a lot of agonizing, that since two of the drawings had been placed in her art box at Philippa, Juliet was in more danger at school than her father in his office or Thomas in his elementary school.

Each day seemed to pass more slowly than the one before it. Every minute became an hour, each hour an eternity. How could this week ever have seemed short to her? "Such a little thing" she had called it. How wrong she'd been!

And each day, anxiety clung to her like the furry cobwebs in her spider nightmare until her brother and her father arrived home safely.

Juliet did shape up as promised. She attended all of Megan's classes, helped around the house, visited Jenny in the hospital, and seemed content to stay home in the evening as long as Justin joined her there, and sometimes Barb and Cappie and Hilary, with whom Juliet had spent twenty minutes on the phone Tuesday morning in apology. Hilary had forgiven her.

There were no more notes.

But Megan reminded herself that the warning in the last drawing, the tom-tom, hadn't been fulfilled yet.

Maybe it wouldn't be. Maybe whoever had been doing such cruel things had repented and given up. That was possible, wasn't it?

Anything was possible.

Wednesday afternoon, Donny Richardson joined them at lunch. Although he said little, nervously tugging on his skinny little mustache the whole time, Megan noticed Juliet watching him carefully. His bright pink shirt gave his skin a yellowish cast, and he chewed on his lower lip while he listened to the conversation.

Why was Juliet watching him like that?

"There's something about him," she told Megan later, at home. "I'm not sure what. Maybe he's just a creep. But I definitely felt something. I'm going to keep my eye on him."

"You think it's him? Hurting people, I mean?"

Juliet shrugged. "I'm not sure. But I'll keep my eye on him, Megan, you can be sure of that."

She would have to, because Megan couldn't add one more person to her list of people to watch. It was hard enough keeping track of three.

When Megan's feeling of isolation became especially overpowering, she tried to focus on the fact that, in spite of everything, Juliet seemed happy with her week. The thought wasn't enough to lift Megan's spirits, but it kept her from drowning in despair. She was glad she was making someone happy, especially someone who had once known her grandmother.

Juliet talked a lot about the changes in the world in forty-six years. Although she was careful not to express amazement around other people, with Megan she was more open.

"You have so many fun things now. Stereos and videos and MTV, and your supermarkets are unreal! When I lived here, the lake was our only entertainment." Juliet shuddered. "I never liked it here, but my father did. He wouldn't move back to the city, even though we were much happier there."

"The accident must have been horrible for him."

"Yes, it was. He was devastated. He loved me very much. And I him." Juliet was silent for a moment. Then she added softly, "I warned him about this place. Martha told me there had been deaths here. But he wouldn't listen." With a regretful sigh, she changed the subject to more pleasant things like compact discs and hot rollers.

Megan's mother continued to improve and was up and around, relieving Juliet of the heavy housework burden. Although that allowed her more free time, Megan's father stuck to his rule about no one leaving the house in the evening.

"Sheriff Toomey hasn't learned anything new," he said when Juliet begged for permission to go out for pizza. "You can order pizza in and eat it here."

"It's so frustrating!" Juliet complained later, sitting on the bed with a pizza box at her side. "I think your father's being silly. Nothing's happened since Saturday night. And I don't think anything is going to. Whoever did all that stuff must have decided it was too risky."

"You don't know that, Juliet. Dad isn't taking any chances, that's all."

Megan felt sorry for Juliet. This week couldn't be what she had hoped it would be. No one was giving any parties, the mall was deserted, and nothing fun was going on in town. Not that Juliet was complaining. She had Justin.

"I told you, Juliet, that this wasn't a good time."

Wiping a blob of tomato sauce off the blue print comforter, Juliet sighed heavily. "I know you did, Megan. But I didn't have any choice. It was either before your birthday or never. Anything is better than never."

"I guess." Megan wished she could believe that Juliet was right about no more harm coming their way. The tom-tom note had been placed in her cubbyhole on Monday. This was Wednesday. If something were going to happen, wouldn't it have happened by now? None of the other drawings had appeared so far in advance.

But she didn't believe for a second that it was over. The sheriff hadn't arrested anyone. Jenny's accident and her mother's attack and Hilary's fall off the catwalk couldn't be dismissed just because there were no clues. There had been someone out

there when those things happened, and that someone was still out there.

But what was he waiting for?

And who would be his next victim?

Megan got her answer the very next day.

Chapter 16

The Logan house, like other homes facing the lake, backed up to the boulevard. An enclosed back porch with a row of windows across its width looked out over the wide street, Thomas's route home from school. It was there that Megan went Thursday afternoon when she realized that her brother was fifteen minutes late.

The tom-tom drawing danced across her mind, taunting her.

I should have gone to school to follow him home. Justin is bringing Juliet, so I was free to leave her, and Dad is still at the office. I could have gone to Thomas's school to make sure he was all right.

Peering out into the drizzle through the faded yellow curtains, she hoped that her mother, peeling potatoes in the kitchen, wasn't watching the clock. If she noticed that her son hadn't arrived yet even after repeated warnings to come straight home from school, she'd become frantic.

Megan saw the truck before she saw Thomas. It was an eighteen-wheeler. They didn't ordinarily come through the village, preferring instead the open highway circling Lakeside. This one must have had a delivery at the mall. It was huge, its cab bright yellow and shiny black. It wasn't going very fast, probably only thirty-five miles an hour. But its size alone made it no match for a skinny little boy on a bicycle.

Afterward, Megan told herself over and over that even if she'd had a voice, even if she'd been able to run, she couldn't have stopped any of it. It happened too fast.

The truck heaved its lumbering bulk around a corner just as Thomas came whizzing down the street. Megan thought he was whistling as he turned the handlebars. It seemed to her that his mouth was pursed when he looked up and saw the truck bearing down on him.

He can stop, Megan told herself. *He has plenty of time. All he has to do is use his brakes.*

He tried. She saw him try. She watched as his hands clenched the brake levers again and again, saw the muscles in his thin arms strain as he squeezed with all his might.

Nothing happened. The new red-and-silver bicycle, Thomas's tenth-birthday present from his parents, never even slowed down. It aimed straight for the mammoth metal truck as if it were magnetized.

Thomas, still pumping the brakes frantically, closed his eyes as the truck loomed menacingly over him.

Sound and time stopped as the truck and the bicycle collided.

And as Megan silently screamed, *No, no, not Thomas!* her brother's skinny little body flew up into the air as if shot from a cannon. It somersaulted twice before slamming back down to the ground, landing on a thin strip of green dividing the boulevard.

People began running out of their houses to gather in horrified silence at the scene. A woman in a blue bathrobe took one look and ran back inside to call for help. The few cars on the boulevard came to a standstill. A man in a gray suit, a woman in a yellow raincoat, and two teenaged boys in sweatsuits left their cars to run to Thomas's aid.

In the kitchen, Megan's mother heard the truck's brakes screaming and instinctively sensed that they had screamed too late. Her eyes flew to the clock. When she saw the time and realized that she hadn't heard Thomas's familiar back-door slam, her jaw went slack, and her hands went to her mouth. She ran to the back porch windows.

Megan, watching in agony, knew the exact moment when her mother recognized the red-and-silver bike lying on the ground. With a half scream, half moan, Connie Logan raced for the back door and out of the house.

There was time for him to stop, to get out of the way. And he used his brakes, I saw him. Why didn't he stop?

Thomas couldn't give her any answers. He was

unconscious, bleeding from the nose. Although the ambulance attendants said nothing as they gently lifted him onto a stretcher and took him away, accompanied by his weeping mother, their faces were grim.

As the ambulance pulled away, Megan felt the same horrible wrenching sensation that had torn at her when she'd entered the mirror for the final switch. What was happening to her family? First her mother, now Thomas.

The sounds of the street, the birds singing as if something terrible hadn't just taken place, the boat motors out on the lake, the small crowd whispering about the accident, it all seemed vague and distant, as if it were taking place at the far end of some long, dark tunnel.

Megan cried soundlessly, seeing Thomas's limp, broken body being lifted onto the stretcher. *You have to be okay, Thomas, you have to.*

Although she needed desperately to get to the Medical Center, she stayed behind to wait for Juliet and tell her what had happened. She was about to go into the house to wait when she saw Juliet standing on the corner, watching the ambulance shriek down Lakeside Boulevard.

"Thomas has been hurt," Megan said quickly, anxious to get going. *"Did you see it happen? Where's Justin?"*

Juliet nodded. "I saw it. Justin had to drop me off at the library. He had some stuff to do there. I walked the rest of the way. How bad is Thomas hurt?"

"Bad. I'm going to the hospital. You'd better come, too."

"I will. I'll call Justin at the library. He won't mind coming to get me when he finds out why."

He didn't. While they were waiting for him, Juliet asked Megan, "Your party won't be canceled now, will it?"

Megan was stunned. *"The party? Cancel the party? Juliet, Thomas could die! You don't think I care about that stupid party now, do you? I don't care if it's cancelled."*

"You don't mean that," Juliet protested. "I mean, maybe you think you do now, because you're upset. But believe me, you'll be sorry later, when Thomas is okay and you didn't get to celebrate your sixteenth birthday. I know how that feels, Megan."

What was taking Justin so long? *"Juliet, I know you were really disappointed about your party, and I'm sorry about that, but I just don't feel the same way you do. Did. Do. I can have a party any time, but I only have one brother."*

When she arrived at the hospital, Megan hovered near her distraught parents, awaiting news of Thomas's condition. Slowly, she went over the accident in her mind. The red-and-silver bike was new. Those brakes should have worked. Why hadn't they? Had someone deliberately destroyed Thomas's brakes the way Jenny's steering mechanism had been destroyed? Or was it really just, a simple, tragic accident?

No. It wasn't. Or there would have been no tom-tom drawing.

Who would hurt a little kid?

Not Vicki. Even she wouldn't do something that nasty.

Unless . . . unless she was totally crazy. Out of her mind.

Because that's what it would take for someone to target an entire family. And wasn't that just what someone was doing?

Megan watched Juliet take a seat beside Megan's mother. *She doesn't belong there. I belong there.*

It seemed years before the doctor arrived to tell them that Thomas would be a patient at Lakeside Medical Center for some time. He had a fractured pelvis, a broken leg, and a concussion. He was out of surgery now and would sleep all night. They might as well go home and get some rest.

Connie stayed, but she sent her husband and Juliet home, telling them they would have to take her place at Thomas's bedside the next day, so they needed a good night's rest.

When they got home, Megan's father went straight to bed, while Juliet checked the answering machine in the kitchen to see if Justin had called.

There were messages from Hilary, from Cappie, and from Mrs. Tweed at Cut It Again, Sam, informing Miss Logan that the operator scheduled to do Miss Logan's hair on Saturday afternoon had taken ill, but another operator could take care of her beauty needs at two o'clock if that would be all right. If not, could Miss Logan please give them a call?

"I told you to cancel that appointment," Megan said.

Juliet shrugged and concentrated on additional messages. "Oh, golly, Megan, I forgot," she said as Justin's deep voice began speaking. "I'll do it tomorrow, first thing, I promise."

Megan didn't feel like listening to Justin tell Juliet he missed her or he loved her or whatever he was telling her these days. All those things he'd never told Megan. She went upstairs, mentally preparing the speech that would put an end to this nightmare. Surely Juliet would understand that with a second member of her family injured, it was now time for Megan to become herself again.

But when Juliet came upstairs a few minutes later, she surprised Megan with, "Wait till you see what I've got!" Swinging the denim shoulder bag over the bed, she turned it upside down and dumped out its contents. Out came six or seven sheets of folded construction paper and a handful of brightly colored crayons.

It took a minute or so for the booty to register. Then Megan said, *"What is this? Where did you get all this stuff?"*

Juliet grinned. "In Donny Richardson's locker. This is the first chance I've had to show it to you."

"Donny? You broke into his locker? Juliet, what if someone had seen you? Someone like Donny, for instance? If he's the one behind all this terrible stuff and he saw you —"

"Megan, I didn't do it as *you*," Juliet said. "I did

it as *me*. So no one could have seen me."

"*As you?*" Megan asked. "*What do you mean, as you?*"

"Megan, I'm still me. I told you that before. I can leave your body if I need to. And I needed to. It was the only way I could check out Donny's locker."

"*You can leave? Where was my body while you were going through Donny's locker?*"

Juliet laughed. "Asleep in the school library with your head down on the desk."

She can leave? Just like that? Whenever she wants?

"Listen, never mind that now," Juliet said. She gathered up the paper and crayons. "I'm going to take this stuff and the drawings you found to the sheriff tomorrow. I figure, if he arrests Donny, things will calm down. And then," she added brightly, "your parents will let you have your party. Especially now that we know Thomas is going to be okay."

"*Juliet, I —* "

"Don't thank me, Megan. My goodness, I owe you so much! This is just my tiny little way of thanking you." Stuffing the colored paper and crayons back into the shoulder bag, she added, "I told you everything would be okay. And it will be. Now I've got to go eat something. I'm starved. Night, Megan."

Her step as she left the room was light and happy.

I should feel like that, too. What Juliet did today,

what she found, doesn't that mean an end to all of this? If the sheriff arrests Donny tomorrow, and why wouldn't he, I won't have to worry about something happening to Juliet before Saturday at midnight. I'll still be here, in this awful place, but it'll only be for two more days and then it will all be over.

So why didn't she feel better? Because she didn't. Not at all.

Chapter 17

When Megan came inside the next morning after a long, lonely night out on the lake, Juliet had already gone.

She must have left early to talk to Sheriff Toomey. Will what she has to show him stop this awful nightmare? It has to!

The room was a mess. There were clothes everywhere, and the closet door stood open. Inside something black and very pink caught Megan's attention.

Megan moved to the closet. Hanging between her new party dress and a pink robe was a short, black, strapless dress with a hot-pink cummerbund and a full skirt. Not the kind of dress anyone wore to a pizza place or the mall or a movie. This was very definitely a party dress.

Where had it come from?

I would never wear a dress like this. It's too sophisticated. More Juliet's speed than mine.

But Juliet wasn't going to the party. If there *was* a party, Juliet wouldn't be going. So why did she need this dress?

Does she have a big date with Justin tonight? Is he taking her some place so special that she had to go shopping?

The date must have been made earlier in the week, because Justin wouldn't suggest a big date with Thomas hurt and in the hospital. In fact, if they'd planned a date, Justin had probably canceled it when he heard about Thomas. Juliet would have to take the dress back.

Megan spent the day at the Medical Center, encouraged by Thomas's condition. He wasn't talking much, lying pale and listless in the bed, but he was conscious. And by late afternoon, he was more concerned about the damage to his bike than his own injuries.

But Megan felt drained and weak. If Sheriff Toomey didn't put Donny away, her father could be hurt next. Tom-tom. Only one Tom was in the hospital so far. Or Juliet could be the next victim. It was lucky that she hadn't been hurt so far, probably because she was always with Justin or Hilary or Barb and Cappie. There really must be safety in numbers.

Hoping for good news, Megan went to school at the end of the day to ask Juliet about her visit to the sheriff's office.

And the first person she saw leaving Philippa was Donny Richardson, unaccompanied by Sheriff Toomey or a deputy, no handcuffs on his wrists. Strangely enough, he looked like an ordinary, lonely boy walking home from high school alone. There was nothing sinister about him.

Bitter disappointment drowned Megan. Why hadn't he been arrested? And with the disappointment, feelings of doubt surfaced. Donny Richardson certainly didn't look like a killer.

But wasn't that how killers got away with their terrible deeds . . . by looking ordinary?

Juliet had found the evidence in Donny's locker. He might look ordinary on the outside, but on the inside he had to be evil.

Still worried, Megan continued to look for Juliet. Unsuccessful at school, she decided to try the house.

No one was there. Each room was silent, still, as if waiting patiently to see what would happen next.

Where is Juliet? Megan's cold, empty world suddenly began to spin around her. Something terrible had happened to Juliet. Something that had stopped her from going to the sheriff. That's why she wasn't at the hospital, wasn't at home. With only one more day left in Juliet's week, Megan's worst nightmare was upon her.

If Juliet is hurt or . . . dead . . . what will happen to me? Oh, God, please don't let me stay like this forever! Please! Let me have my life back again!

Juliet could have gone straight to the hospital from school. Racing over there, Megan prayed, *Be there, Juliet, be there!*

She wasn't.

But Sheriff Toomey was.

When Megan saw him, she was terrified. Had he come to tell her parents that the body of their daughter had been discovered, lying in a field somewhere? *I will never be me again. This horrid, empty world is all I'm ever going to know, because Juliet is gone, and I can't switch back now.*

"So," the sheriff said to Thomas, "you're saying you couldn't stop? That you tried and failed?"

He was there to talk about Thomas's accident.

The darkness lifted around Megan. The sheriff was there about Thomas, not Juliet. All hope wasn't lost.

A pale, bruised Thomas nodded. "Is my bike okay?" he asked anxiously. "It's practically brand-new, you know. Mom says you guys took it to check it out. Is it okay?"

The sheriff smiled. "Sure, son. Your bike'll be fine. One of my deputies took it over to Mickey Ryan's bike place. He can fix anything. It'll be good as new in a couple of days."

"Yeah," Thomas grumbled, "but it'll never be the same. Darned truck."

When the sheriff asked Megan's parents to come outside and speak to him, Megan followed.

In the corridor, Sheriff Toomey shook his graying head. "Go figure," he said. "The guy in the truck says he tried to stop and couldn't, just like your son. We're looking into it, but I don't expect we'll find anything more than we found in the Winn girl's accident. Or your accident, Connie. No leads, no clues." Another grim shake of the head. "I remember, thirty, forty years ago, when your mom was young and theirs was the only house out there on the lake. Owned twenty acres. Everyone else lived in town. Martha told me they never locked their doors or windows, not even at night. No reason to." He let out a weary sigh as he turned to leave. "Times sure have changed."

He never said a word about crayons or drawings or warnings of any kind.

Why had Juliet changed her mind about telling him? And where *was* she?

She was home, Megan discovered when, desperate, she returned to the house again. A wave of relief washed over her when she moved into the bedroom and found Juliet rummaging around in the closet.

"Juliet, where have you been?" Megan demanded. The terrible things she'd imagined happening to Juliet during the past few hours had nearly driven her crazy. *"I've been looking all over for you."*

"Justin and I went for a ride."

"A ride? You knew I was waiting to hear what Sheriff Toomey said, and you went for a stupid ride? I thought something terrible had happened to you."

Juliet laughed. "Well, I'd scold you about your overactive imagination, but if you didn't have an imagination, you probably never would have heard my voice in the first place."

Megan had been too terrified to be so easily placated now. *"You should have gone to the hospital after school. Mom and Dad could use some support."*

"I was there first thing this morning. Thomas seemed so much better, I decided to come home and rest up for my date with Justin tonight. We were going out to dinner downtown."

The black dress.

"But Justin decided that wouldn't be such a hot idea, with Thomas in the hospital. So we're going over to the Medical Center for a while and we'll check in on Thomas and Jenny. Then we're going to Justin's house. Cappie and Barb and Hilary are coming, too, I think. It'll be fun."

"Juliet, did you talk to Sheriff Toomey? What did he say?"

"Oh, Megan, he wasn't even there. I rushed right over there when I got up this morning. Didn't even eat breakfast. But he wasn't there, and his deputy was talking on the phone for hours. If I'd waited, I'd have been late to school, and you told me not to cut any more classes. I went back again after classes, but he wasn't there then, either."

He'd been at the hospital.

"Juliet! This is not a simple shoplifting crime we're talking about! My friends and my family have almost been killed! It can't wait! The only reason I didn't tell you last night that we had to switch back right away was you let me think Donny would be arrested today. Now you tell me you haven't even seen the sheriff yet. So nothing has changed, Juliet, nothing at all. You're . . . I'm . . . we're still in as much danger as we always were. Something could happen to you at any minute, and that would be the end of me. You said so yourself."

Hearing the intensity in her voice brought fear to Juliet's eyes. She still had one more night and day. "Megan, think a minute. Thomas is in the hospital, and your parents are safe there, too. They're staying the night, they told me so. And I'll be safe at Justin's house. Nothing more is going to happen tonight. I'll see the sheriff first thing tomorrow, I promise. And by the way, Megan, this should cheer you up. The party is still on."

"It is?" Megan asked, surprised.

"Yes. Isn't that wonderful? Your mom said she wanted to show the whole village that the Logans weren't going to be intimidated. She said it would do everyone a world of good to have a party. And Thomas would still be in the hospital, asleep, by the time the party started, anyway."

"I still can't believe it," Megan said.

"Well, it was your mother's decision to 'carry on' as she said."

Megan was silent for a minute as Juliet looked into the closet for an outfit for that night.

"Juliet, where did that dress come from? The one right there in the closet? Black, with pink trim?"

"Oh, Megan!" Juliet cried, "you are such a snoop! I bought that dress for you as a surprise, and now you've spoiled it."

"I have a dress." Juliet had said the same thing about the hair appointment, that it was for Megan. But Megan hadn't wanted her hair done any more than she wanted the black dress. Juliet knew the dress wasn't her type. *"I don't need another dress."*

"Megan," Juliet said firmly, "after all the work I've done with Justin this week, you're not going to blow it by showing up at your party in a dress as juvenile as that green one, are you?"

"You said it was pretty. Before, in the mirror, you said it was a great dress."

Juliet shrugged and began digging through the pile of shoes on the closet floor for a suitable pair. "It's okay, Megan, but it's not very . . . interesting."

Interesting? She meant sexy. *"Juliet, I'm not wearing that black dress to my party. I'm wearing the one I picked out. So you can take that one back tomorrow."*

"Oh, all right. But I think it's gorgeous, and I think you're crazy." Her words drifted off as she unearthed the shoes she wanted and slipped them on.

It's hard to believe she and my grandmother were friends, Megan thought. *They aren't anything alike.*

While Juliet was dressing in the white skirt and a royal-blue short-sleeved sweater, Megan remembered Sheriff Toomey's remark about her grandmother's house being the only one on the lake forty years ago. Then where had Juliet lived?

"Juliet, where did you live? When you lived here, I mean? Was it on this street?"

Before Juliet could answer, the telephone shrilled.

"Oh, hi, Cappie," Juliet said when she'd picked up the receiver. "You're going to be at Justin's tonight, aren't you? The only reason my folks are letting me out of the house at night is I'll be where there are lots of people and two of them, Justin's parents, are grown-ups." She wrinkled her nose in distaste. "I guess it's better than nothing."

Megan was swept up in a wave of overpowering envy. Maybe a night at Justin's surrounded by friends was only "better than nothing" to Juliet, but it sounded wonderful to her. She couldn't wait to be back in that world again, *her* world. Only one more night and one more day . . .

Megan didn't remind Juliet that this was her final outing. Why ruin it for her?

Hearing the arrival of her parents downstairs, Megan went to see how her brother was. Juliet could be on the phone for hours.

According to her parents' conversation, Thomas was doing much better, but Connie still intended to return to the hospital as soon as she'd showered and changed.

The idea of her father being alone in the house until Juliet came home later only made Megan more anxious. Anything could happen. *I can't keep an eye on both Dad and Juliet when they're in two different places. Why didn't Juliet invite everyone over here? She knows how worried I am about the tom-tom drawing.*

Megan hurried upstairs, intent on asking Juliet to call everyone and switch the gathering to the lake. That way, her father wouldn't be in the house alone.

But she was too late. When she entered the room, it was empty. Juliet was gone.

Chapter 18

Megan spent a long, lonely night, not leaving the house until her father went to bed. Even then, she stayed in the den for a while, waiting for Juliet and thinking.

Only one more day . . . and then she'd be herself again. Thank goodness nothing had happened to Juliet so far. It was a miracle, really, that she was still okay. And by this time tomorrow night, the whole awful week would be over — nothing more than a horrible memory. If only Sheriff Toomey would arrest Donny — then the horror really would be over.

Tiring of waiting for Juliet, Megan left the house, assured that her father was safe in his bed, and went out to roam the lake.

This is the last time I'll ever be able to do this, but I won't miss it at all. I'm not a bird or a bat, and I shouldn't be flitting around out here with them — especially when so much is wrong in my own world.

It was very late when she returned to the house.

Juliet was in bed, sound asleep, her clothes in a pile on the floor beside the bed.

Megan was disappointed. And surprised. She hadn't expected Juliet to be able to sleep at all, knowing that she had only one more day. *If it were me, I'd spend the time until morning walking along the lakefront, maybe with Justin, waiting for the sunrise, squeezing the juice out of every last minute.*

Thinking that surprised Megan. It didn't sound like her. It sounded like . . . someone who wanted to fill up every minute of life with interesting things, instead of withdrawing from it by living in a dream world.

Maybe that's because I'm so terrified that I won't get to do those things ever again. That something will happen to keep me from doing them. Maybe that's why I feel different.

When morning finally arrived, Megan was torn between a ferocious anxiety on this last day and a tentative sense of relief. It was almost over. Almost.

Juliet went to see the sheriff as promised, and Megan went with her. He wasn't there. The deputy in charge said he would be back around dinnertime, which seemed to Megan eons away. But there was no choice other than to wait.

I should be getting good at that. But I'm not.

When they returned from running errands, they found Megan's father up on a ladder on the stone terrace, stringing brightly colored lights above the lakefront lawn.

Since Juliet was safely home, Megan concentrated on keeping an eye on her father. When he climbed down from the ladder to get a glass of iced tea in the house, she followed. Juliet wasn't in the kitchen or the living room. Megan searched the first floor thoroughly. No Juliet. She hadn't gone out again, had she?

Anxiously Megan went upstairs and into the bedroom.

Juliet was lying on the bed, her eyes closed, legs straight, arms at her sides. She was wrapped in the white terrycloth robe. The shades were drawn, the room dark, lighted only by a cluster of short, squat candles on a blue metal tray on the nightstand.

Dumbfounded, Megan thought, *What is she doing? What are all these candles for? It looks like a séance. Is she taking a nap on her last day? That doesn't make any sense.*

Candle shadows flickered across Juliet's face, giving it an eerie yellow-gray glow. She was lying so perfectly still. Not a finger curled, not a muscle twitched, not a lash blinked. Her skin looked smooth and waxen, like the face of a department store mannequin.

Suddenly there was a startled shout from the terrace. It was immediately followed by the sound of shattering glass, a slam that shook the house, and then silence.

Juliet sat bolt upright, wide awake, and jumped from the bed. "What was that?"

Megan flew to the terrace, with Juliet right behind her.

The ladder had fallen. The upper half of it had thrust itself through the big picture window Megan's father had installed less than a month ago. He was lying on his back in the midst of shards and slivers and chunks of glass. A gash on his cheek bled profusely, and his hands and sandaled feet were measled with red. But he was conscious and seemed more abashed than pained.

"Dad," Juliet scolded, rushing over to help him up, "you shouldn't be up on the ladder in sandals. It's dangerous."

"No kidding." He got up very carefully. "But . . . it wasn't my fault. The ladder just . . . tipped right over."

A pensive Megan watched from a distance as Juliet helped Tom Logan douse his wounds with antiseptic and bandage those that needed it. Megan couldn't help feeling that something very weird was going on. Had Juliet really been asleep when that ladder fell? She hadn't looked asleep. People didn't look like that when they were sleeping. They looked relaxed. Sometimes their mouths hung open and their bodies got all loose, as if their bones had been removed.

But Juliet had been as stiff and rigid as a piece of wood. Like . . . a statue or a slab of cardboard. Like . . . there was no one in there.

She said she could leave my body any time. When she left before, it was to look through Donny's locker. What was she doing this time when she left? When the ladder fell? Where did she go? Someplace far away? Or . . . only as far as the terrace?

Worry and suspicion began to gnaw at Megan. Wasn't it just a bit too coincidental that the ladder had fallen at the exact moment when Juliet didn't seem to be in Megan's body?

But that was crazy. Juliet had no reason to harm Megan's father. Why would she?

She wouldn't.

I'm being ridiculous. It's all this tension, trying to get through this last day.

But the worries wouldn't go away. Megan watched Juliet wash her father's wounds with a soft rag. *Juliet was never worried about something happening to her,* Megan thought. *I worried about that all by myself. And I thought that was because she couldn't be hurt physically. Because she had already lost her life and had nothing to lose.*

Then Megan thought of something else. *She can leave my body so easily. She can go anywhere, do anything, without leaving a trace. No fingerprints. No one can see or hear her. There would never be any witnesses because Juliet would be invisible.*

Megan thought about the night of her mother's accident. Juliet had been with Justin in the den, watching a movie. Megan had watched movies with Justin more than once. He became completely lost in them. Several times, Megan had left to get popcorn and drinks, and he'd never even noticed her absence. It would only have taken Juliet a second to leave Megan's body and dart out to the dock to attack her mother. Justin wouldn't even have noticed that the girl beside him was as quiet and motionless as a doll.

Maybe Juliet knew all along that no disaster would befall her because . . . because she *is* the disaster. *Think about it*, Megan told herself. *Makes sense, right?*

No. No! Juliet couldn't have done those things. It's not possible.

Juliet helping Megan's father made a nice picture: the loving daughter taking care of an injured parent with tenderness.

Was it fake? Had Juliet herself *caused* those wounds?

No, she couldn't have, Megan realized. *She couldn't have done any of it, for one very good reason. She had waited too long for this one short week of life. She would never have deliberately set out to wreak havoc on her precious seven days.*

But look at her! Think, Megan, think! Does she look like someone whose time is almost up? Is she nervous? Depressed? Is there a look of dread in those eyes?

No. Not at all. Juliet is as calm and peaceful as the lake at night.

Juliet finished her nursing duties and, warning Tom Logan to "stay away from ladders," ran lightly up the stairs.

The dark, devilish thought, once born, became relentless. It crept up on Megan steadily, like the big, black, hairy spider of her dream. It circled around her, teasing, taunting, wrapping her in its web.

The dress. The black dress with the pink cummerbund. The hair appointment.

They hadn't been intended for Megan. They had been intended for Juliet.

Because Juliet had never meant to have only one short week. She had never planned to give back Megan's life.

She was going to keep it for herself.

Juliet was going to have her birthday party after all.

Juliet had tricked her! Right from the beginning . . .

Megan raced up the stairs and into the bedroom.

Why? Why would Juliet do this? She had sounded so sad and sweet in the mirror, so full of yearning.

But she had done terrible, vicious things.

Why?

Juliet looked up when she felt Megan enter the room. The blinds were still closed, the flickering candles providing the only light.

"You know, don't you?" she asked calmly. "You've guessed."

"Yes. But I don't understand any of it."

"You want to know why? Is that why you're here?"

"Yes."

Juliet settled back on the bed, her skin yellow-gray from the candle shadows. Expressionless, she said, "Then I'll tell you. Why not? It's too late now for the truth to do you any good."

Megan waited.

"It's because of Martha."

"Martha? My grandmother?"

Juliet nodded. The candlelight transformed her eyes into glowing, greenish-yellow coals. "Yes, Martha, your grandmother."

Again, Megan waited.

"She was my stepsister."

Chapter 19

There was a long silence before Megan said slowly, *"That's not true. My grandmother only had one stepsister. Her name was Etta. She died three months after my great-grandmother married her father."*

"*Etta!*" Juliet spit the word out with disgust. "I am *Juli*etta. My new stepmother — your great grandmother — said my name was too fanciful and ordered everyone to call me Etta. Horrid name! But my father said I had to respect my stepmother's wishes." Juliet's voice was her own again.

"I don't believe you."

"I was fifteen when my father married Lily Lewis." Juliet's upper lip curled in a sneer. "I hated her on sight. I hated Martha even more, her and her stupid brothers!"

Megan's mind was reeling. *"Why did you hate them?"* she whispered.

"Because we didn't need them. We didn't need anyone. I told my father when my mother died that I'd take care of him." Juliet's voice lifted, became happier. "It was wonderful for a long time. I was my father's hostess when he entertained. I had beautiful dresses to wear, and everyone treated me as if I were grown-up. Then," her voice hardened, "we came here on a vacation and he met that horrible Lily. We moved here, to this awful place, and everything changed."

In shock, Megan spoke slowly. *"That's why you never told me where you lived. You lived here, in this house! I wondered when Sheriff Toomey said there weren't any other houses out here that long ago."*

"I hated this house. A country house, boring and dull. I was used to living in the city. Nobody here knew anything about museums and art galleries and theater. Instead of dinner parties, they had picnics!" Her voice oozed contempt.

"I've seen pictures of my great-grandmother. She was very beautiful."

Agitation made Juliet's voice erratic. Her sentences came in spurts. "She was shameless . . . chasing him. A widow, with three children to support . . . she knew a good thing when she saw it. I tried to warn my father that she only wanted his money, but he wouldn't listen to me."

"He must have really loved her."

"Love? Love?" Juliet screamed, her features sharpening, her skin draining of healthy color. "We didn't need her or her dull, stupid children. But he married her, and we moved to this awful house and that horrid lake." Her voice lowered, became edged with bitterness. "He never had any time for me after that."

"No one has ever talked about that time very much," Megan, completely stunned, murmured. *"I knew you died, but I never knew how or why. No one ever said."*

"Well, of *course* they didn't! If *you* had killed someone, would your family talk about it?"

Megan gasped. *"Killed? You said it was a boat accident that took your life."*

"It wasn't the accident that killed me!" Juliet shouted. "Our boat hit a rock and we were both thrown overboard. But the crash didn't kill either of us."

"Us?"

"Martha and me."

The candles flickered as the wind, growing stronger every minute, rattled against the closed blinds, as if knocking to get in.

"I was struck unconscious. But Martha wasn't. She wasn't hurt at all. She could have saved me. But she didn't. Your sweet, kind grandmother," Juliet said with hatred, "clung to the side of the boat and watched while I sank like a stone. And then she watched me drown."

"She wouldn't have. Never."

Juliet jumped up from the bed and began a wild pacing, back and forth across the faded blue carpet. There was nothing in her face now that resembled Megan. Her skin was dirty-white, her mouth pinched and twisted, and thin strands of her hair traced a spiderweb across her cheeks.

Megan watched in disbelief. She doesn't even look human anymore, she thought, and wondered how she could ever do battle with such a creature. Because it was clear now that, to save herself, she was going to have to fight Juliet.

But *how?*

"You can't have my life, Juliet. I won't let you."

"She stole *my* life!" Juliet cried. "She hated me as much as I hated her." Her eyes grew colder. "I would never have got into that boat with her, but my father insisted. He said it was my fault she was lonely. He implied that I had stolen all of her friends."

"I think you did," Megan said softly. *"I think you hurt her because you were jealous when your father found a new family."*

Outside, the wind began to pick up speed. It blew across the lake with a low moaning sound that penetrated the walls of the bedroom, bringing with it a chilly dampness.

Juliet's eyes began to glow yellow like the candle flame. "I don't care what *you* think! But I cared what my father thought. I hated Martha for turning him against me. And I told her so. In the boat, when we were out on the lake where my father couldn't hear."

"You fought with her?"

"I told her I hated her. Martha said some terrible things to me. I ordered her to turn the boat around. She refused." The heels of Juliet's sandals dug into the carpet with each angry step. "I tried to take the oars from her. But she fought me. Then we hit the rock."

As she neared the window, the wind-tossed curtains whipped around her, shrouding her in white lace. "And Martha let me drown."

"I don't think so. I think she tried to save you. You couldn't have known, because you were unconscious. I think you hate her so much, you don't want to believe she tried."

Juliet turned away from the window, lace still coiled around her neck and shoulders. She ripped it away from her. *"She* was the one who should have died! I was the pretty one, the popular one. Dull old Martha with her books and her piano and her bird-watching, *she* got to live!"

Then, before Megan could respond, Juliet stopped her pacing and faced the big oval mirror. "But it's all right now. It is. I'm getting even, at last. You've seen for yourself that I, too, can hurt people, just like Martha hurt me." She smiled an evil smile. "Your mother never knew what happened to her. Neither did Hilary."

"You did it all? Everything?"

"The car accident, Thomas's bicycle, your father's ladder. Even the drawings. I did every bit of it. And loved doing it."

"But why us?" Megan asked, bewildered. *"My friends and family never did anything to you. Jenny, Barb, Hilary, they never even knew you existed. Why did you try to kill them?"*

"Because *you* care about them. And Martha cared about *you*. I never had the chance to pay *her* back. Until you moved in. I knew she loved you. And I knew I could take my precious revenge on you and your family and friends. It was even better that way."

"We never did anything to you," Megan cried angrily. *"And I don't think my grandmother did, either."*

Juliet's face contorted in rage. "What I've done is simple justice. Your grandmother loved you. I couldn't punish her, so I punished you. You love your friends and family. Not one of them has remained untouched. Can't you see that's justice?"

"You let me think it was Donny. Or Vicki. You wanted me to think that. And they hadn't done anything. It was all you."

"They didn't matter. They're unimportant. And now you, your grandmother's favorite person, will take my place, in *my* world, and I will take yours. Forever. That, too, is justice." She smiled vaguely, her anger gone. "You know, Megan, it is uncanny how much you look like her." She laughed wildly, a sound that rocketed off the walls and slammed into Megan. "Isn't that funny? I'll spend my whole life looking exactly like the woman I hate most. Are you laughing, Megan? Don't you think that's funny?"

Frozen in shock, Megan heard the back door slam. Her father was returning to the hospital to be with Thomas and her mother.

"Now," Juliet said briskly, "I have to get ready to go out. Justin broke our date because of your silly little brother's accident." She giggled. "I'll have to go find Justin, won't I?" Her face began to rearrange itself into Megan's features. Her voice became Megan's again. "You do get it that the only reason Justin wasn't hurt is that I want him for myself, don't you? I'm going to take very good care of him for you, I promise."

Megan, shaken to the core, watched as Juliet went to the closet to pick out an outfit. Fighting to gather her senses together, Megan said in an unsteady voice, *"I am Megan, and I want to be me again."*

Nothing happened.

She said it louder, *"I am Megan, and I want to be me again!"*

Still nothing.

"Forget it," Juliet said calmly. "I left out one very important detail when you agreed to switch. Remember when I said your consent was necessary for the trade? Well, so is mine. That's fair, isn't it? I guess I forgot to mention that part. It's supposed to be an honor kind of thing. You give me your life for a week, and I give it back, willingly." She laughed. "Only I seem to have misplaced my honor. Can't find it anywhere." Her face twisted in anger again. "I guess I lost it when I drowned in that lake, thanks to your grandmother."

Holding up a red leather skirt and examining it carefully, Juliet said, "What do you think your chances are of getting my willing consent to switch back before midnight tonight, which happens to be all the time you have left?" Her laugh this time was almost a cackle. "I'd say that's about as likely as Justin wishing I were you again."

"*Juliet, you can't!*" Megan shrieked. "*You can't do this. You have to give my life back to me. You can't keep it!*"

"Just watch me!"

A dizzied, tormented Megan watched in revulsion as Juliet preened before the dresser mirror. *That's my face, my body . . . and no one will know that the inside of it is evil and decay, like rotten fruit.*

"*Juliet, you had your week. I gave that to you. You can't pay me back for that by stealing what's mine.*"

"Oh, yes I can. And I'm going to."

Satisfied with her appearance, Juliet moved to the door. "See you, Meg," she said cheerfully. Then she stopped and slapped herself lightly on one cheek, laughing. "What am I saying? I won't be seeing you at all, will I? As of midnight, you're history."

"*I'm not leaving, Juliet,*" Megan promised grimly. "*I'm not giving up. I'll get back what's mine before midnight.*"

Juliet's laugh was scornful. "Don't try to scare me, Megan. You're no match for me. At midnight, the clock in the den downstairs will go *bong, bong,* twelve times, and you will disappear like a puff of smoke. Forever." She grinned. "Better you than me."

"*Juliet, stop! Wait! Please, you can't —* "

"Kind of like Cinderella." Juliet opened the door. "Except that you won't turn into a pumpkin. You'll turn into . . . nothing. Absolutely nothing!"

"How can you be so evil?" Megan cried. *"I hate you!"*

The smile disappeared. The eyes became cold, green glass. "It isn't me you should hate, Megan. You should curse the day Martha Lewis was born. As I have cursed it for forty-six years."

Alone in his room, Justin had been thinking about Megan. He was probably being loopy minding the change in her. Most guys would have been wild about the new, livelier, more affectionate, girl he was spending so much time with these days.

But the truth was, he missed the "old" Megan. The one he could talk to about anything while she listened, and always understood. The Megan who never flirted with other guys, and was nice to people, and cared about her family.

What had happened to that Megan? Hilary blamed it on raging hormones, due to a sixteenth birthday coming up fast.

Then Justin remembered a comment Megan had made a few days ago. Had that been last week? Or this week? What was it she had said? "Something weird is going on at my house." And she'd said more than that, too. Something about death . . . if only Justin could remember what it was. Maybe then he'd understand why she'd changed. Or why all those horrible things had started happening to her family.

What had Megan said? And why hadn't he listened?

Justin sat up very straight in the hard-backed wooden chair. Megan's best friends, her mother, her brother, all had been hurt. Why hadn't he realized that she could be next?

Justin jumped to his feet and ran out of the room.

Even as Megan reeled in shock and terror, she was conscious of the time passing. There wasn't much left.

The only thing Megan knew for sure was that she wanted her life. Juliet couldn't have it. It didn't belong to her. And Megan was going to get it back.

But how?

Juliet had said she had to give her consent for the reverse switch. How would she ever get it? Megan tried desperately to concentrate, but she was so frightened. And the clock on her dresser ticked away stubbornly.

Juliet would have to give it up. Willingly. What would make her do that?

Think, Megan, think! There has to be a way! Juliet would obviously never give up out of the goodness of her heart, that was for sure. No, Megan would have to do something to make Juliet *want* to let go. She'd have to scare her. But what was Juliet afraid of? Then Megan remembered the scene at Lickety-Split, when Justin had suggested a boat ride.

The lake. Juliet was terrified of the lake.

How terrified? Enough to make her leave Megan's body willingly to escape the deep, dark water?

And how would she get Juliet out on that water?

She'll never go near it. Not for me. I can't make her go out there.

But . . . was there a chance she'd go out on the lake with someone she liked and trusted? Someone she liked being alone with? Someone like . . . Justin?

Megan's mind raced. *Was it possible? But how would I communicate with Justin? Juliet didn't say I could. Still . . . we both have open minds and we're such good friends. . . . And he acts like he's in love with Juliet, which means maybe, maybe he's in love with me. It's worth a try. If only I can find him before Juliet does.*

Megan went in search of Justin.

Justin made it to the Logan house in ten minutes flat. No one answered his ring. They were probably at the hospital with Thomas.

It was late. They'd be home soon. He'd wait. He really needed to talk to Megan.

Justin went down and sat on the dock. To wait for Megan.

Chapter 20

Megan found Justin sitting on the dock behind her house. The wind had died down, and the lake was empty of boats. Everything was peaceful and quiet, as if nothing were wrong. But it was — terribly wrong. What if Justin wasn't able to hear her?

She'd be lost. At midnight, she would disappear forever.

He has to hear me. He has to! Oh, please, please, Justin hear me!

"Justin, it's Megan. Can you hear me?"

The moon made little silver ripples on the water, a boat's motor died somewhere in the distance, and an owl called out a question, but Justin didn't move. His long legs dangled over the dock, and he trailed a long, thick branch back and forth in the water. He gave no sign that he had heard Megan.

"Justin, please *hear me! It's important! I'm right here. Open your mind and listen.*"

Justin lifted his head, tipped it slightly. But he said nothing.

"I can't do this without your help. You have to hear me, Justin. It's me, Megan."

This time, Justin looked around. Although he saw nothing but water and darkness he *felt* something. Megan was near. He knew it. "Megan?" he said tentatively. "Where are you?"

Sudden warmth enveloped Megan. Justin had felt her presence. There was hope. "Yes, Justin, it's me. I know you can't see me, but I'm here. All I want you to do is listen. Will you do that, Justin?"

He continued to peer into the darkness. There were lights all along the shore, some from docks, others from houses close to the water. But as the moon took refuge behind a cloud, the darkness thickened.

"Even if we had lights," Megan explained, "you wouldn't be able to see me. So just listen!"

"If you're hiding," he said, "you'd better give it up. I'm not in the mood for games."

"I'm not hiding, Justin, I promise."

Justin climbed to his feet. His mouth looked grim. "I don't get you, Megan. Playing games after everything that's happened. Doesn't seem like you." He uttered a short, harsh laugh. "But then, lately you just don't seem like yourself. I miss the old Megan, the one I knew so well."

"You still know me well, Justin, or you wouldn't be able to hear me."

"It's so strange, Megan. I know you're here — I can feel it." Justin's eyes explored the dock area. "But I can't see you anywhere."

Through an open window, Megan heard the

grandfather clock in the den strike the quarter-hour. Quarter past eleven. She had exactly forty-five minutes to explain this whole thing to Justin and enlist his help in getting rid of Juliet. That couldn't possibly be enough time.

"I'm not hiding, Justin. I promise. I need to tell you something. You're going to find it very hard to believe, but you must. My life depends on it. And you know I'd never lie to you, not ever."

"Megan," Justin said slowly, "does this have something to do with what you were trying to tell me a few days ago — about the strange things going on in your house?"

"Yes, Justin."

"I wish I'd listened to you then," Justin said as he sat down on the dock. "Well, I'm ready to listen to you now. And I hope it's not too late."

"So do I," Megan agreed. *"So do I."*

Telling him the story was harder than Megan had imagined. When she'd traded with Juliet, she had believed she was doing the right thing. How could she have known that Juliet was deceitful, vengeful . . . *evil?*

"The reason you can't see me, Justin," she began, *"is that . . . I've traded places with a . . . with someone who died . . . a long time ago."*

"What?"

"I know, I know how it sounds, Justin, but please, just hear me out. It's really important that you listen and that you believe me."

"You traded places with a . . . ghost? Is that what you're telling me? Megan, come on. Quit kidding around. I'm in no mood for this." The disbelief in his voice chilled Megan.

But she had to keep trying. *"It's true, Justin. She was my grandmother's stepsister. She showed up a week ago, in that old mirror in my bedroom, and she asked me to trade places with her for one week. At first I said no. I was scared. Terrified. But she kept begging me. I started to feel sorry for her."*

"You were talking to a ghost in your mirror? Megan . . ."

"Just listen to me, Justin, please. She said that all she wanted was one week. And after I'd thought about it, one week didn't seem like so much. It seemed like such a little thing. And she was so sad and seemed so sweet."

"A little thing? To give your life to somebody else?" Justin's voice held amazement, but the disbelief was gone. He could hear the urgency in her voice, and he trusted her. "Why didn't you tell me? I guess you tried to — but I was too worried about Jenny's accident to pay any attention."

"I wanted to tell you everything. But I couldn't. She said not to tell anyone. I thought she was sweet and nice, and it wouldn't hurt to give her just one little week out of a whole lifetime. Does that . . . do you think that's crazy?"

Justin sat in stunned silence. "I knew there was something . . . but this . . . I'd never have guessed this." He shook his head, his eyes focused on the water.

"I thought Juliet was gentle and good, and I felt

149

sorry for her. But she isn't. She's evil. She did all those things . . . caused all the accidents — Jenny's, Hilary's, my mom's, Thomas's. She hated my grandmother, and she's getting even. That's why she's here.

"Anyway . . . we were supposed to trade back tonight at midnight. That's what she told me. But . . . but Juliet never intended to. She was lying the whole time. I just didn't figure that out — until today."

"But, Megan . . . what does that mean?"

"It means . . . that if I can't find a way to force her to switch back before midnight tonight, Juliet will keep my life, and I'll be trapped in this horrible place . . . forever."

Megan had told her story. There was nothing more to say. She could feel the seconds ticking away, her time running out. Would Justin believe her?

Justin sat silently for a long moment. Then he said, "So, how are we going to make her switch back?"

He was going to help. He believed her, and he was going to help. "Oh, thank you, Justin! Thank you!" But there was still a battle ahead of them, Megan thought. "The only thing I could think of was this: Juliet is terrified of the lake. It's where she died. Remember that night in Lickety-Split when you talked about a boat ride? Remember how scared she got? I thought, if we could get her out on the lake, maybe she'd be so frightened, she'd leave my body. *That's what has to happen. She has to leave it willingly.*"

Justin stood up, but he didn't know where to look. The sound of Megan's voice came from all around him, not just from one place. "What do you want me to do?"

"*You have to find her, Justin. Right away. There isn't much time left. I'll help look for her. And I'll stay with you the whole time, but I'll have to be careful. If she senses that I'm with you, she'll know there's something wrong, and you'll never get her out on the lake.*"

There were no boats on the lake now. It was quiet, as if it had gone to sleep for the night. Justin looked out over the black water. "If she's that afraid, what makes you think I can get her out on the lake?"

"*You can do it, Justin. I know you can. Promise her a special romantic boat ride, just the two of you in the moonlight. She loves being alone with you and she loves romance. It's our only hope.*"

"You think she'll agree to it?" Justin's voice was doubtful.

"*Her fear of the lake is the only thing I know for sure about Juliet. So I don't have any other plan if this one doesn't work. That's why it has to work. I know the two of us together can beat her. I know we can!*"

The determination in her voice weakened Justin's doubts.

"Come on, then," he said, and added with a won-

dering laugh, "wherever you are. Let's go get Juliet
and offer her a nice midnight boat ride."

"Before *midnight*," Megan warned as Justin began running up the slope toward the house. *"Midnight would be too late."*

Under the terrace lights, Justin glanced at his
watch. It was eleven-thirty. Drawing in a quick
breath of alarm, he began running faster.

And ran into Juliet as he rounded a corner of the
house. He almost called out her real name in surprise but caught himself just in time.

"Justin!" Juliet cried, obviously happy to see him.
"I've been looking all over for you! This town is
completely dead tonight." She made a face of disgust. "They're all a bunch of scaredy-cats. There
was absolutely no one at the mall, so Cappie and I
went to a movie. The theater was practically empty.
And no one was eating pizza, either." A note of
petulance crept into her voice. "Where have you
been, Justin?"

Megan, staying a safe distance away, saw Justin
struggle to speak. It was one thing to listen to a
story about Megan changing places with Juliet, and
something else to be staring at the proof.

*Snap out of it, Justin! There's no time for that!
And if you're not careful, she'll guess that you know
something. Remember the boat ride. Get her down
to the dock. Hurry!*

"Hey, gorgeous," Justin said then, throwing an
arm around Juliet's shoulders, "I was looking for
you, too. I've got a great idea. Your folks aren't

home. I checked. So how about if you and me take a little boat ride, just the two of us? I know this great little island on the other side of the cove. . . ."

Caught off-guard, Juliet pulled away from him, backing up against the house. Her eyes were wild with fear.

Good. That's a start. I want her to be afraid.

"I've . . . I've got a terrible headache, Justin," Juliet stammered. "I came home to get some aspirin and go to bed. I don't want to be all puffy-eyed for my party tomorrow."

Justin pulled her close to his chest. "I thought you said you were looking for me," he said softly.

"Well, I was. The headache just came on, a minute ago. It's a real killer, honest."

"Oh, come on, Meg. Just the two of us. A nice, quiet boat ride out to this little island I know is just what you need."

Juliet shook her head. "No, honestly, Justin, I can't. I told you, I don't like the lake anymore. My mom — "

"Oh, your mom's fine," Justin said impatiently. "You're being silly." He reached down and tipped her chin up toward him. Smiling down at her, he said, "Megan, I thought you were really growing up this week. You seemed so different, like you were ready to stop being Mommy and Daddy's little girl. But if you're afraid to be alone with me . . ."

Juliet hesitated. Megan knew she was thinking that being Megan wouldn't be nearly as much fun if she didn't have Justin. "Why can't we be together inside?" she whispered. "You said no one was home."

Hurry, Justin, hurry! Make her quit stalling!

"Megan," Justin said firmly, "I am going for a boat ride. If you won't come, I'll find someone else who will." He paused, then added, "Vicki loves the water."

The den window was open. Breaking the stillness, the chime signaled the quarter-hour.

Fifteen minutes! I have only fifteen minutes to get rid of Juliet. That isn't nearly enough time! She's going to win. Oh, no, she can't! She can't win!

Justin softened his voice. "A moonlit boat ride," he said softly, holding Juliet close. "What could be more romantic?"

Without waiting for an answer, he placed a firm grip on Juliet's elbow and began leading her down to the dock. When they reached it, she pulled back. "There's no moon," she complained, her voice shaking. "What fun is a midnight boat ride without a moon?"

"It's just hiding behind a cloud. It'll come out in a minute." Justin grinned. "It's waiting for you to make up your mind. C'mon, let's go!" He jumped into the motorboat and held out his hand to Juliet.

But she hung back. As Justin started the motor and the lantern came on, Megan could see that Juliet's face was pale and strained. She was chewing on her lower lip.

"Megan, what's with you?" he said, deliberately layering each word with suspicion. "You're looking at this boat like it's a two-headed monster. You're acting really weird."

Then there was one long, scary moment as Juliet debated with herself. Megan could see her wavering between her horror of the lake and her determination to hold onto Justin. She didn't want to lose him now, now that she thought she *owned* Megan's life.

Megan waited. *She's thinking the boat ride will be a short one. She's thinking that it's not as if she actually has to go into the water. And she's wondering just how much fun my life would be without Justin in it.*

"Nothing's more romantic," Justin said softly, "than two people alone on an island at night."

Juliet stepped into the boat.

Chapter 21

Juliet took a seat, her hands clenched into tight little fists, as Justin started the motor.

"You'll love this place, Megan," Justin said soothingly. "It's very private."

"I can't stay long." Her voice was nervous. Her eyes swept the lake as the boat picked up speed. Megan knew she was searching the water for rocks, although there were none in this open part of the lake. "It's late, and I've got to get some sleep so I'll look really good tomorrow." She was sitting stiffly on the seat, her hands gripping the sides of the boat. "You haven't forgotten my party, have you?"

My *party, you mean*, Megan thought angrily. She remained a cautious distance behind the boat, fearful that Juliet would sense her presence.

The boat began to veer toward the cove.

Juliet's body shot up straight in her seat, propelled by alarm. "Justin, what are you doing?" Anxiety made her voice shrill. "There's no island over there. Just the cove."

"Have to go through the cove to reach the island," he said cheerfully. "There's a little opening off to one side. Relax, Megan, we'll be there in no time."

"No! I don't *want* to go to the cove! I hate that place!"

Justin half turned his head to look at Juliet. "Since when?" he said, a hint of mockery in his voice. "I thought you loved the cove."

"I don't. It's too dangerous. People die there."

"Tell you what," he told Juliet calmly, "I'll just scoot around the edge, okay? We'll be there in no time. Relax."

Megan could see Juliet fighting with herself. Megan was worried. Her plan wasn't working. They'd been on the lake for a while, but Juliet hadn't given up.

And there were only ten minutes left.

Would being in the cove — the rocky, treacherous spot where Juliet had lost her life so long ago — be enough? Would that scare Juliet away forever?

What if it didn't?

Hurry, Justin, hurry! Megan cried.

Justin sped up the boat, aiming straight for the cove.

Juliet jumped to her feet. "Justin, you lied! You're not going around it! You're going in there!" Her voice, filled with alarm, rang out above the noise of the motor. "Slow down! What are you doing?"

Leave, leave now, Juliet! Megan screamed silently. You know you want to. Do it! Give my body back to me! It's mine!

"Justin, turn this boat around, right now! I want to go home!"

It's not your home, Juliet, it's mine. And I want it back. Leave!

"Sit down," Justin ordered Juliet. "Sit down before you fall down."

"Justin Carr, I demand that you turn this boat around right this minute! It's cold out here, and it's getting windy. Take me home!"

She was right about the wind. In just minutes, the trees lining the shores of the cove were bending low against powerful wind gusts, and the surface of the water was churning and boiling. Gray clouds flew past the moon, and the boat began to pitch and toss. Juliet moaned and sat down, clutching the sides of the boat, her face distorted with a terrible fear. The choppy water slopped up into the boat, drenching both of them.

"Justin!" Juliet screamed against the wind. "Please!"

Megan felt new hope. There was desperation in that voice. That was what Megan had been waiting for.

Megan decided it was time to let Juliet know that she was there. Learning that Megan and Justin had planned this together, that Justin knew the truth, might be exactly what was needed to send Juliet over the edge.

There were only five minutes left. She had to try.

"Juliet, I'm here. It's me, Megan."

Juliet's head snapped up, her hair sodden now. She jumped to her feet, awkwardly straddling the bottom of the boat. "No! You can't be here! Go away!"

Justin continued to steer the boat, at high speed, straight toward the cove.

"I can be and I am. This little excursion was my idea."

Juliet, battered by wind and spray, peered into the darkness. "That's impossible. You can't communicate with Justin. I'm the only one you can talk to."

"That's not true. Justin and I think alike. We both have open minds, and Justin has a kind heart. You said that was all it took, remember?"

The boat sped the last few yards into the cove.

"Stop him!" Juliet screamed, teetering dangerously. "I can't go in there! I can't!"

"Then don't. Leave. Leave now. Leave willingly, Juliet."

And for one small, agonizing second, Megan thought it had worked. She could feel Juliet's frantic need to flee, to escape the place she hated and feared so passionately.

But in the next second, a violent, ugly rage replaced the fear. "It's not that easy, Megan!" Juliet screamed. "I'll turn this boat around myself!" And in one sudden, fierce movement she leaped at Justin and began clawing at him, struggling to gain control of the boat.

"Turn it around!" she screamed, pounding at his

hands. "I'm going back! And you can't stop me!"

Justin, fighting against the sudden attack, lost control of the boat. Megan watched in helpless horror as the small craft rushed straight ahead through the churning waters. . . .

. . . And slammed into a rock looming like a glacier above the surface of the lake.

Upon impact, Justin was knocked backward to the floor of the boat.

But Juliet, with a blood-curdling scream, was catapulted up into the air and then down, down, down, into the boiling black water waiting below.

Chapter 22

Justin pulled himself to his feet. The sound of Juliet hitting the water paralyzed him for one shocked second. He stood in the motionless boat, frozen, as she disappeared from sight.

The boat's lantern had been dislodged during the collision with the rock and now floated aimlessly an inch or two beneath the surface of the water. Battery-powered and waterproof, it cast an eerie glow over Juliet as she resurfaced, thrashing about violently.

Justin saw her trying to scream as water flooded her mouth and nose.

Megan's mouth. Megan's nose. He drew in a sharp breath. That was *Megan's* body drowning.

Justin poised himself on the edge of the boat, preparing to dive into the lake. The violent wind raked at his long hair, tore at his body.

"No, you can't!" Megan cried. *"Justin, you can't save her. Not yet. She has to leave my body willingly. She'll do it, any second now. I can see it in*

her eyes. She can't bear to be in the water. We have to wait."

Hearing Megan, Justin paused. But, watching Juliet thrashing about in the wind-blown water closing around her, he thought, What good will it do if Juliet leaves, but Megan's body is lost forever?

And, although Megan cried out, *"Stop, Justin, no!"* he could see no other choice. He dove into the wild, dark water.

Desperation seized Megan. She had gambled on Juliet's absolute terror of the water to make her abandon Megan's body. But being in the boat hadn't done it. And now being in the water wasn't doing it. Juliet was still in there, and only three minutes remained.

Why was Juliet still struggling? Why hadn't she given up?

Then the answer came: She was fighting, still, because she believed that Justin would save her. *She doesn't know he's not a good swimmer — that he'll never be able to get to her. She thinks she'll be free of the water in a minute or two, so she's hanging on.*

Megan felt time racing by. It was too late. She had gambled and lost. There was no more time.

I am drowning now, she thought in despair. *My life is ending, there in the water. And so is Justin's, because there will be no one to save him.*

No. That is not going to happen! We're going to live our lives, Justin and me. Juliet isn't going to rob us of the time that's ours. I want it! I want my life! And I'm going to get it back from her!

And so Megan went to Juliet, who was going under for the second time. Justin was trying to reach her, but the wind had whipped the water into a fury, and although he struggled valiantly, he was losing the battle.

Submerged, the light from the lantern surrounding her with a sickly yellow-green glow, Juliet's features became misshapen, grotesque. Her eyes were wild with panic.

"Give me back what's mine," Megan demanded. *"Justin can't save you, Juliet. The wind is too wild. The current is too strong. You're going to die here. Again."*

Juliet answered her mentally. *You're lying. It's not true.*

"Listen to me! HE CAN'T SAVE YOU! No one can. And my body is dying and will do you no good now. Give it up. Give it back to me."

Justin came up for air, gasping, his eyes wild. He began fighting again to reach Juliet. Foundering, he grasped her collar. With a massive, supreme effort, he heaved her up out of the water, straining desperately to grasp the side of the boat. He failed, and they both sank.

In her mind, Megan heard the grandfather clock beginning to strike midnight. *Bong, bong, bong, bong . . .*

"Juliet, you've lost." Then she began repeating, *"I am Megan, and I want my body back. I am Megan, and I want my body back. I am Megan, and I want my body back. . . ."*

Juliet's eyes had become deep sockets of glowing

yellow. "No-oo," she wailed, "no-oo. My party, my party . . ."

"No, Juliet. It's my party. And there won't be a party, if you drown. I am Megan, and I want my body back. I am Megan, and I want . . ."

The glowing eyes closed in despair. *No party? No party? Justin will not save me?*

"No, Juliet, he can't. You are drowning. Again. Just like before."

Bong, bong, bong, bong . . .

Juliet's mouth made a round O of agony. *Me-gan! Here it is! Here is your body. I give it back to you willingly. I have no choice. I cannot stay here in this terrible place. Take it, and know that you will never see me or hear me again.*

Then her lips twisted and from them came a bellow of rage so despairing, so filled with anguish and torment, every creature within hearing distance shivered with fear. Animals hid in burrows and tree branches and bramble bushes, and people in their houses on the lake slid deeper beneath their bed coverings, taking refuge from the obscene sound.

Bong . . . bong . . . bong . . .

With a joyful relief so overwhelming it made her weak, Megan reclaimed her body as the wailing Juliet left it.

Bong.

As the blood-chilling cry echoed out across the lake then slowly, slowly, trailed off into silence, the feeling of weightlessness left Megan and she found herself in the water, supporting an exhausted Justin. The wind softened to a whisper, the lake became as still and subdued as a pond.

"It's me, Justin," Megan gasped. "It's really me. Juliet is gone. Forever."

Justin was too drained to do anything but nod weakly.

Helping each other, they struggled into the boat, and lay in the bottom, breathing hard and shivering with cold, but relieved.

After a while, Justin reached out for Megan's hand. They linked fingers. Although their flesh was clammy and cold, each took warmth and reassurance from the other's grasp.

When she felt her strength returning, Megan got up and found two blankets in a metal chest under one of the seats. Then, wrapped in gray wool, she tried the motor. It coughed, choked, and started.

Justin stood close beside her as she backed up the damaged boat and turned it away from the cove. Then he put an arm around her.

"Someday," he said quietly, "you can tell me the gruesome details. I want to know all of it. But right now, let's go home. We're going to a very important party tomorrow, remember?"

Megan smiled and nodded.

She aimed the boat toward home, exhausted but happy, as the moon slid out from behind a bank of gray clouds and began shining down on the dark, peaceful water.

And only the wildest of the forest creatures continued to hear the echo of a despairing, tortured wail in the soft whisper of the wind.

About the Author

DIANE HOH is the author of *Funhouse*. She grew up in Warren, Pennsylvania, "a lovely small town on the Allegheny River." Since then, she has lived in New York State, Colorado, and North Carolina. Ten years ago, she and her family settled in Austin, Texas, where they plan to stay. "Reading and writing take up most of my life," says Ms. Hoh, "along with family, music, and gardening."

point ® **THRILLERS**

R.L. Stine
- ☐ MC44236-8 The Baby-sitter $3.50
- ☐ MC44332-1 The Baby-sitter II $3.50
- ☐ MC45386-6 Beach House $3.25
- ☐ MC43278-8 Beach Party $3.50
- ☐ MC43125-0 Blind Date $3.50
- ☐ MC43279-6 The Boyfriend $3.50
- ☐ MC44333-X The Girlfriend $3.50
- ☐ MC45385-8 Hit and Run $3.25
- ☐ MC46100-1 The Hitchhiker $3.50
- ☐ MC43280-X The Snowman $3.50
- ☐ MC43139-0 Twisted $3.50

Caroline B. Cooney
- ☐ MC44316-X The Cheerleader $3.25
- ☐ MC41641-3 The Fire $3.25
- ☐ MC43806-9 The Fog $3.25
- ☐ MC45681-4 Freeze Tag $3.25
- ☐ MC45402-1 The Perfume $3.25
- ☐ MC44884-6 The Return of the Vampire $2.95
- ☐ MC41640-5 The Snow $3.25
- ☐ MC45682-2 The Vampire's Promise $3.50

Diane Hoh
- ☐ MC44330-5 The Accident $3.25
- ☐ MC45401-3 The Fever $3.25
- ☐ MC43050-5 Funhouse $3.25
- ☐ MC44904-4 The Invitation $3.50
- ☐ MC45640-7 The Train (9/92) $3.25

Sinclair Smith
- ☐ MC45063-8 The Waitress $2.95

Christopher Pike
- ☐ MC43014-9 Slumber Party $3.50
- ☐ MC44256-2 Weekend $3.50

A. Bates
- ☐ MC45829-9 The Dead Game $3.25
- ☐ MC43291-5 Final Exam $3.25
- ☐ MC44582-0 Mother's Helper $3.50
- ☐ MC44238-4 Party Line $3.25

D.E. Athkins
- ☐ MC45246-0 Mirror, Mirror $3.25
- ☐ MC45349-1 The Ripper $3.25
- ☐ MC44941-9 Sister Dearest $2.95

Carol Ellis
- ☐ MC44768-8 My Secret Admirer $3.25
- ☐ MC46044-7 The Stepdaughter $3.25
- ☐ MC44916-8 The Window $2.95

Richie Tankersley Cusick
- ☐ MC43115-3 April Fools $3.25
- ☐ MC43203-6 The Lifeguard $3.25
- ☐ MC43114-5 Teacher's Pet $3.25
- ☐ MC44235-X Trick or Treat $3.25

Lael Littke
- ☐ MC44237-6 Prom Dress $3.25

Edited by T. Pines
- ☐ MC45256-8 Thirteen $3.50

Available wherever you buy books, or use this order form.

Scholastic Inc., P.O. Box 7502, 2931 East McCarty Street, Jefferson City, MO 65102

Please send me the books I have checked above. I am enclosing $_____ (please add $2.00 to cover shipping and handling). Send check or money order — no cash or C.O.D.s please.

Name _____

Address _____

City_____ State/Zip_____

Please allow four to six weeks for delivery. Offer good in the U.S. only. Sorry, mail orders are not available to residents of Canada. Prices subject to change.
PT1092

point

Other books you will enjoy, about real kids like you!

☐ MZ43469-1	**Arly** Robert Newton Peck	$2.95
☐ MZ40515-2	**City Light** Harry Mazer	$2.75
☐ MZ44494-8	**Enter Three Witches** Kate Gilmore	$2.95
☐ MZ40943-3	**Fallen Angels** Walter Dean Myers	$3.50
☐ MZ40847-X	**First a Dream** Maureen Daly	$3.25
☐ MZ43020-3	**Handsome as Anything** Merrill Joan Gerber	$2.95
☐ MZ43999-5	**Just a Summer Romance** Ann M. Martin	$2.75
☐ MZ44629-0	**Last Dance** Caroline B. Cooney	$2.95
☐ MZ44628-2	**Life Without Friends** Ellen Emerson White	$2.95
☐ MZ42769-5	**Losing Joe's Place** Gordon Korman	$2.95
☐ MZ43664-3	**A Pack of Lies** Geraldine McCaughrean	$2.95
☐ MZ43419-5	**Pocket Change** Kathryn Jensen	$2.95
☐ MZ43821-2	**A Royal Pain** Ellen Conford	$2.95
☐ MZ44429-8	**A Semester in the Life of a Garbage Bag** Gordon Korman	$2.95
☐ MZ43867-0	**Son of Interflux** Gordon Korman	$2.95
☐ MZ43971-5	**The Stepfather Game** Norah McClintock	$2.95
☐ MZ41513-1	**The Tricksters** Margaret Mahy	$2.95
☐ MZ43638-4	**Up Country** Alden R. Carter	$2.95

Watch for new titles coming soon!
Available wherever you buy books, or use this order form.

Scholastic Inc., P.O. Box 7502, 2931 E. McCarty Street, Jefferson City, MO 6510₂

Please send me the books I have checked above. I am enclosing $ _____
Please add $2.00 to cover shipping and handling. Send check or money order - no cash or C.O.D's please.

Name _____

Address _____

City _____ State/Zip _____

Please allow four to six weeks for delivery. Offer good in U.S.A. only. Sorry, mail orders are not available to residents of Canada. Prices subject to changes.

PNT4